E<small>nd</small> O<small>f</small> T<small>he</small> W<small>orld</small>

BY: DRAEGON GREY

- Draegon Grey is the author of 'Worlds'
and the soon to be published 'Rise of Davian'.
He lives on the west coast and enjoys spending
his free time writing stories for others to enjoy.

FST PULP
P.O. Box 64051
San Francisco, CA 94164, U.S.A.

First Edition - FST Pulp Printing, March 2011

Edited by Cheryl Rice Jones

-O-

Many, many moons ago, long before man was even imagined as a blink in the immense stratospheric minds of those with immeasurable power, whose very presence was beyond any known explanation, forces were waiting to control everything that was to come. It was ab aeterno once the first life blinked into existence and from that instant, a battle seemed to be brewing. It was then that the one who possessed control over all beings decided that another of the powerful should pay the ultimate price – banishment for his greediness.

"I did nothing to deserve exile," thought Norevilania, who was the second most powerful being in existence. "I will get my revenge; I will soon be the one who is ruling. Let him see what it means to be banished."

Beings known as Etherials roam the sky constantly in peace and harmony. They always glide effortlessly over the terrain of green and blue. Time being of no consequence to them, they enjoy the beautiful exhibition of light, and they bring joy to the skies which are already glistening with colors of blue, yellow and green, cascading ubiquitously. The scene seemed to underline serenity, ensuring constant happiness and joy to all who existed there. Just the possibility of banishing a colleague caused that light to fluctuate, the only time it ever had. Sorrow permeated the peace and harmony for a brief moment. Everything was a part of the unknown. They didn't know how to react; it was all so new. One could hear murmurings and grumblings. It was more than not knowing what it meant. It was an embodiment of the unknown. To them, it was actually the seeds of chaos.

Reacting to the confusion, Almightanius, quickly brought equilibrium back by changing the confusing new hues back to the standard blue, yellow and green. Soon, peace and harmony returned.

Filled with anger, resentment and the deepest hatred he had ever experienced, Norevilania believed it would take a bit of time, something actually akin to eternity to get out of this new and barren place of torture, darkness and wretchedness where he had been so cruelly banished. He would have to use every tool at his disposal to make changes. He would exclude nothing.

It wasn't long until Almightanius was content with his newly amassed power, but he soon sensed that something was missing and pondered. *"Why should we be the only ones to experience this existence? We should create a being that could enjoy the peace and harmony. Existence wouldn't be programmed. It would be an experiment. We could instill in them the ability to make choices. Then Norevilania would be satisfied, too. It would be a kindness to him. He could have subjects and perhaps then he will be satisfied. They'll be like us, but with no extraordinary powers. Their powers will be potential. It could be easy for them to make choices. They could have control over their outward appearance. It might be a challenge to keep them balanced. But, the cocoon desired one thing – equilibrium. The cocoon should have our form. We will make him and a companion and place them in the Luminose atmosphere. There they can prosper and exist in peace and harmony. To help them exercise their power, we will place a beautiful vine with colorful flowers, mixed with edible leaves. They will be instructed that they should avoid contact with the vine. If they ignore the warning, it will show they do not deserve to remain in peace and harmony. This behavior would be an outward indication that they might prefer the unknown outcome of experimenting with their own desires to the tried and true – the known consequences that have been striving for peace and harmony. That was step number one.*

Banished from the kingdom to a place of total darkness and hatred, called Hethanos, Norevilania sat on his self-made throne of red stone. He was sulking – actually it was more like burning with hatred. The few, –two of them, banished along with him because of alliances that had been embedded since the beginning of his banishment– watched and waited for his command. They offered suggestions of a multitude of retaliation modes. He listened to their ideas, and then he responded.

"No, You idiots. What are you thinking? None of that is going to work! Look around. I am down here in this wretched place, while he enjoys the comforts of his illustrious kingdom. He thinks he will appease me with the creation of beings. But, will they listen to me? Whoopie doo! He has probably made them his robots anyway. But, I will use these beings he created against him. It won't be long before everyone of them will be my ally, and then he won't have any power," Norevilania droned in his loud deep, and today, exceedingly whiny voice.

When Norevilania was banished, at that same moment, a man and his companion emerged on another amazingly serene and beautiful day. It was on a hillside, just steps away from the Etherials. The man looked to be as perfectly physically developed, as his companion. Both had smooth light skin and softly textured long curly hair. It was clear though that the companion was a female. It was her perfectly cut long hair and round plump breasts and all those majestic curves that distinguished her from the chiseled masculinity of the broad shouldered man.

The two gazed at each other amazement. Their physical attraction was obvious. The man gazed at his companion with a fire that didn't need additional fuel to telegraph his need for intimacy. It was etched in his face. His loins transmitted an urgent message of need. She felt it deep within her, too. She accepted his offering, an echo of that primeval throb that for her was a need to experience his manhood inside her. The two of them were a vision of unadulterated sexual passion. They became one after an embrace that actually broadcasted crystal colors of pink and purple rays, flickering into the atmosphere like fine dusting powder flung into the wind. Etherials gazed in amazement at the colors, not sure of the significance, having never seen those fleeting, but vibrant hues before then. Inexplicably, they had gathered to watch – en masse.

Pleased with his creation, Almightanius had sent the man and his companion to planet Earthios where only they would be in residence. He etched two words into the core of their being – "make more." They did.

Not too far in the future, Almightanius filled Earthios with numerous beings. They appeared to be of varying races, colors, sizes, shapes and beliefs. What he called "man" grew tremendously in a multitude of ways. One result of the metamorphosis was that the being was making choices with unexpected outcomes. There were consequences. If a being were unable to show care and compassion for others when it seemed required, or if one was singularly concerned with itself, it would mean banishment to a dreadful place, with only one outcome.

Soon after the man and woman came together on Earthios, there was placed a flower that should they touch it, the automatic gift of roaming with Etherials would be taken away. Now the humans would have to prove themselves worthy. Could humans do it? Could they control themselves even with the influence of his companion or with the others? Only time would telegraph that response.

Over time Norevilania did get subjects. Now many men and women were part of his ever-growing empire. He took out his frustration and anger on his subjects using the greatest torture, making his territory unbearably hot. He refused to let go of the hatred and resentment. He wanted retribution for what he thought Almightanius had done. He constantly blamed everyone around him for it. However, this was not enough. He would never stop.

The message was clear – REVENGE! Whatever it took.

-1-

Man had evolved and so had his technology. Just as here on Earth, the Internet became a way to interact, virtually. It could do what one would normally do in person. It became a popular activity. Everyone possessed a computer, which now was just a little box. It was universal – young, old, women and men – everyone was connected. Computers even got smaller as technology advanced. People became more and more savvy in their usage of the Internet.

As man continued to make advancements, Almightanius smiled a new smile, as he mentally recounted the long list of their accomplishments. Norevilania, on the other hand, was in a godly snit. He actually relished the fact that his kingdom was growing, but in his opinion, man was not making the choices Almightanius had envisioned.

Norevilania was always angry. He made frantic calls to his henchmen who weren't equipped to make choices. They obeyed his every whim. They had no capacity to disobey. Norevilania was strong-willed. He was the cheerleader of doom. It was a way to use man's frailties to his advantage. He would use something to stimulate man's desires. It would have to be something that would be hard for man to resist. And he was excited, the plan would call the daemonic to action.

Daemonics were like drones in a beehive that served only their Queen. They served Norevilania. They did his bidding without question. They were workers who had no mind of their own. They were unyielding reflections of the evil one.

One of the daemonics possessed more than malevolent skills. He could create a machine. It was a secret. He knew it would infiltrate the Internet on Earthios. It was while monitoring man's activities, that another of Norevilania's daemonics noticed something else of interest. If the word "evil" were spelled out on the keyboard, something would happen. It was a most curious anomaly. When working to seek more and more internet information, the demoniac saw that when he used the word, "evil", many sites would open and more and more doors would open and then, more still. It seemed as if his quest for information could go on without end. It hadn't been like that before. It was exhilarating.

Norevilania was a novice when it came to the information age. He had no ability to use the Internet. The curious aide, though, –a.k.a., a daemonic–, typed the word "evil" again and again, as he tapped into more and more a sites. Again and again it worked. Knowing what Norevilania wanted, the demoniac went to him with what he had found.

"Can we do anything? How can we make man do what we want them to?"

"Let's see," said Rage, the appropriately named Demoniac.

Rage was at the machine he built. He directed the mechanism to go to a website. The site came into view. It was strange, yet somehow thrilling that he was able to view a young man sitting at a computer. Rage launched a message to the 24-year-old man – Get off the computer!

The recipient of the message had blankly stared at the computer, and then slowly, he had proceeded to turn it off. Norevilania had bristled on the sidelines with a smirk. That sneer turned quickly to an outburst of power. "Yes! He will finally be paying! We must do it quickly before Almightanius finds out that we have this ability. We have to make sure we get to everyone! We need to be in complete control before Almightanius is even. I want him to grovel at my feet before I destroy the world. Almightanius will bow down to me!"

Soon after, on a cold evening, outside a large two story Victorian house, Rage, who was epitome of wickedness, was peering through the bedroom window of Julius, a 17-year-old, black clad teenager, who could have been a Goth if he were living on Earth. He was tall and lanky with dyed long straight hair black. He always wore dark clothing. Julius sat in his room, pecking on his computer as usual. As an only child, Julius spent every evening sitting there surfing the web after he finished his homework. It was a request from his parents. He acquiesced, did his schoolwork, and as usual, when he finished, looked up the unusual sites. They had references to power. He was always planning to be in charge. He wanted to be the most powerful.

He continued surfing through screen after screen, when he decided on a new word to research – "evil". He wondered what would show itself on that screen in front of him. More than mere definitions of "evil" begin to appear. Then a page that seemed unusual showed itself. It was one that really piqued his interest. The screen displayed:

"Wouldn't it be cool to have incredible power? You could be where you should be – on top of the world. Everyone could be waiting for your command. Everything you ever thought you wanted or needed could be at your fingertips. Visit a site that will show the way – www.eotw.com."

Julius became intrigued and excited. He wasted no time clicking through to the link. The browser begins to load the page. After what seemed an eternity, the page finally popped up, startling Justin. On the screen appeared the silhouette of a skull with a wide-open mouth. There was a crown in the background behind a fire that was burning. Justin's appeared to be in a trance as he gazed at the screen, and then still in the trance, slowly reached out to turn it off. The screen powered down, but Julius remained seated, staring at the screen. After a few minutes, he shook his head. It was as if he was returning to reality after a daydream. Shaking off the effects of the stupor, he then came to the realization that his computer had been turned off.

Audibly, he murmured, "I don't remember turning it off. What is happening?"

Rage knew. He knew so well that Julius' internal balance that had been tenuous at best anyway, tipped for a final time. It was power. It was evil. It was more than just a website creeping quietly, but quickly into the computer world of wayward souls who traveled the super information highway. It was looking as if it could lead anyone straight to hell. It was lethal.

-2-

As usual, Michelle was leaving the Manhattan building where she worked. She was headed home to fix dinner for her fiancé. Michelle blended into a crowd. She was 28, and had brown hair and brown eyes. A month ago, she had moved from the Midwest to work as a paralegal for a law firm. Each night, she walked through the park in Union Square heading home to Greenwich. She reached the park, listening to music on her iPod. She entered through the north end. Visions of the delicious food she would prepare for her man, Zak, permeated her thoughts. She was only vaguely aware of a crowd in the park on the warm night. The air was filled with a faint odor of cannabis being smoked by some of those relaxing and enjoying the scenery in the oasis in the middle of the metropolis.

She reached the middle of the park, passing a bench crowded with people enjoying the evening. Three men, totally immersed in the hazy hypnosis of their smoke stare as Michelle glides past them moving to the rhythm of her own music. Without thinking, one of them, a tall scruffy-faced young man sitting mid-bench, experienced a strong desire for sexual pleasure as he imagined what the curves that he could see through Michelle's clothing might reveal if she was naked. Consumed by passion and desire, he ignited that vision and passed it to the other two, who were sharing the bench. Without a word or a plan, the three men decide to follow her. There were no inhibitions, nor direction. It was as if an unseen puppeteer was controlling them.

Michelle had reached a point in the park where very few people remain for very long. It was a small space – maybe a hundred feet square. The three men, still quasi-hypnotized, realized their opportunity was about to expire. They picked up the pace and closed in on her. Michelle, for the first time in many months began to sense something didn't fit into her usually comfortable world. She changed her focus for just a moment, dragging herself away from the energizing beat flowing through the ear-buds into her ears. Surreptitiously, she began looking around as she tried to conjure up the source of her uneasiness. Along with her newly found alertness, she picked up the pace of her stride ever so slightly not wanting to telegraph her fear. She realized that she would soon be shed of the park. Just then, she saw three men dressed in dark clothing walking briskly toward her. Her pace quickened to match her pulse. Something primal in her sensed the danger, too. Each breath she took became quick, as the three dark shadows moved far too close.

As the terror inside her grew, she remembered instructions that at the time had seemed silly. Zak had insisted that if she felt in danger, she was to call or text him with a 911. By then, her pace had increased to an unadulterated speed walk. She reached for her cell phone and dialed. That done, she walked faster still. It wasn't quick enough though. One of her pursuers grabbed her from behind. His left hand enveloped her mouth, pulling her close to him, stifling any sound; ultimately silencing her like a lion squeezing the life from its prey. His other hand grabbed her around the waist and Michelle desperately tossed and flailed her arms in a desperate bid for freedom. Being stronger, he easily held her, willing her body into submission, slowing her efforts enough to finally subdue her. Now she was nearly still. It was then that the other two assailants caught up and joined with the attacker.

Hysterical, she watched as a burly man walked by as if oblivious to her unbelievable situation. She was frantic. She asked herself, *"Is he blind?"* Her attackers were disrobing her. Almost as if watching the scene from afar, she wondered why they were tearing her beautiful two-piece suit. The tallest of the three was behind her. He pulled her down. Somehow she had gathered all of her strength and she managed to bite the stifling hand that suppressed her screams. The attacker's hand left her mouth; but only for a moment. It allowed her to croak in a scratchy, unfamiliar voice. "Take my purse. There is three hundred dollars inside. Let me go! I am begging you." Now, she was completely disheveled and fear had overtaken her being.

A woman in her mid-twenties, dressed in blue and pink sweats ran by the horrific scene. She had her headphones on and there was sweat bubbling on her forehead. She jogged along with her brunette ponytail flapping like a metronome to the beat of her pace. She turned her head slightly to the left, sensing movement somewhere on the ground in the dim light. Her music had muffled Michelle's screams. There was nothing left to recognize of the once beautiful woman. Fear had taken over every feature. The blue and pink sweats avoided involvement. She increased her speed, turned and focused inward. She heard only her music and she knew that she needed to finish the run. She feared for her own safety and was blissfully ignorant of others'.

The attackers were laughing hysterically; all the while ripping and tearing Michelle's blouse to shreds, piece by piece, like an unwanted piece of paper. As if under an incredible spell, two other walkers strolled through the horrific scene. The attackers continued to rip and tear at her. It was as if a doll's clothing was being shredded by an out of control three-year-old. No one responded as the young woman carried out the struggle for her life.

While that situation played itself out, on the other side of the country, a mob had gathered. They stood outside a two-story brick, Victorian home hoping for justice. A skinny, tall, psychotic looking blue-eyed man in his forties was screaming, "You'll never take me alive! Get away from my house! I'll take each and every one of you out, police or no!"

Inside the house were his family – his wife and two children – a boy four and a girl, three. In the bedroom, were his wife and son; both of them were bound. The young boy's face had deep red blotches on his left cheek. It was evidence of his having been abused. It was his father. He was angry all the time.

The enraged man's daughter was distraught. She had matted blonde hair. Her anger matched her father's. Anxiety had forced her to pull her hair out in chunks. The man's wife was in agony because she had refused to follow her husband's demands. She was in the bedroom unconscious. She was crumpled on the bed with both arms broken. They had been injured above her elbows and again at her wrists. The mad man stood behind his front door armed and ready to pull the trigger with any movement from the curious gallery that was gathering outside, to observe the unfolding scene.

As if in a trance, he had moved close to the windows, hiding behind the pale colored curtains that covered them. He was poised to take out one of those annoying people standing outside his house. At least twenty people were standing, posed with the bravado of a crowd, outside his door. They were screaming for his head.

Finally, the police arrived. There were at least forty of them. They were in riot gear, ready to squelch the disruption. The officers were loaded with batons, semi-automatic weapons, smoke bombs, shields, and face and body masks. The crowd wasn't pleased. Many incongruous sounds filled the air. It was a curious mixture of clapping, and booing.

"Back up! Back up!" one of the officers shouted, using his bullhorn to order the crowd to disperse. We'll take it from here!"

The crowd reluctantly began to move. One by one, they began walking away, heading south down the street. There were only a few stragglers.

"They are leaving Mr. Williamson, you can come out now!" carefully, but softly, yet sternly said the one of the shielded cops. Come out and let's talk!"

"No, never, you are all liars! They brought this on themselves!" Williamson responded, angry at the commotion. –He was speaking of his family. The bullhorn speaker thought it was the mob.–

The amplified voice said, "They are leaving now. There is no need to continue this. Come on out so it can be over. It's really all over now!"

"What are you talking about?" Mr. Williamson shouted. "They haven't gone anywhere!," he said while he walked from the front door toward the living room. He stopped at the brown chair and looked at his daughter. She was normally a blue-eyed longhaired blonde sweetie to him. Clearly now, she was not the same girl who could bring sunshine with her smile and brighten any room. She looked as if she had been depressed for a long time. She seemed despondent. There were deep shadows under her eyes from days of constant crying.

"Why is daddy doing this?" she mumbled, only to herself. As soon as the last word that she had forgotten were said aloud, exited her mouth, her rage-filled father's gaze caught her eyes. Almost simultaneously,

"Don't say nothing," was followed by a stinging backhand to the left side of her face.

"Oh daddy," she pleaded through tears seeping uncontrollably out of her eyes.

"Shut up or you'll get another one!" snapped her father.

The tears had turned into quiet sniffling in an effort to avoid more brutality.

While Williamson was confronting his daughter, police officers moved to surround the house. Five to ten officers quietly passed behind parked cars headed to the back of the house. As they reached their carefully orchestrated positions, the negotiator attempted to distract the determined man in the house. It was a ploy to make certain Williamson was unaware of their positions.

"So do we have a deal? You come out and we won't come in," the mediator carefully intoned through the bullhorn.

Inside, the mad man stopped in the doorway to the bedroom. He saw his wife and son just where he had left them. The wife on the bed and the little boy tied to the redwood rocking chair. The wife was unconscious. His son was curled awkwardly in the chair in the fetal position, making no sound, but the tears literally flowed down his cheeks.

"They haven't gone!" he yelled.

"They are exactly where they're supposed to be! Come on out!" the negotiator then almost volleying information, hoping for a response.

"They have to pay!" returned the father. "After that, then I will come out! They deserve this!"

"They deserve what?" asked the cop. "Who is it that you are talking about?"

"You know who I'm talking about. Don't play stupid with me! Don't you fuck with me! I will kill them! I will kill them all!" had come the response from Mr. Williamson.

The dregs of the crowd had heard the exchange. After being strongly encouraged by an officer to disburse, the ranting of Mr. Williamson had enraged a bystander. The situation was combustible. Much to the chagrin of the negotiator, the bystander had begun to holler.

"Let them go, you bastard! You are fucking crazy!"

This was not a good day. Somehow, through the walls of the house, Williamson had heard. He had shouted from inside, "Who'n the fuck are you?"

It was a scene out of an elementary school playground,

"Make me" "I will blow your head off," came the response. It hadn't mattered who said what. It was an escalating situation searching for direction

The negotiator had quickly ordered two officers to subdue the new irritant, the angry man who was reaching into his left pocket pulling out a .357 Magnum. He had planned to shoot into the air, just to hear the noise of it. Two beefy officers tackled him just as the bullet left the chamber.

The large window in the front of the house was shattered as the bullet found its course, penetrating the back of the soft cloth seat Mr. Williamson's daughter was occupying. Luckily, she had tilted her head just as the bullet pierced the chair. The bullet missed by a scant ten inches. Mercifully, the little girl had fainted. Mr. Williamson thought the police were shooting at him. He ran back to the bedroom screaming all the while,

"You'll pay! You did this!" Then he shot his wife.

"Daddy!" the son wailed, just before the bullet silenced him too. His head fell to the right.

Mr. Williamson ran to the living room shooting carelessly, not caring where the bullets traveled. He arrived in the room's entrance spraying bullets left, right and center. Everything in the room, including his lifeless daughter was riddled with bullet holes from the rampage. After actually seeing his daughter dead and bleeding, Mr. Williamson fell to his knees, trying to bury his head in his hands.

His mind seemed suddenly clear and he realized who was lying there. He reached down to push away the matted hair from her bloodstained face. Then the bullets were coming from all directions. The bullets filled his body, causing it to shake as if he was having a seizure.

The gruesome scene was a response by the police to Williamson's rampage. They took cover from the bullets and shot at the house; never taking aim, just shooting until there wasn't a sound to be heard from inside the house. Rage was watching. He was pleased at the chaos that was brewing. He was excited by the smell of dying flesh. He laughed in excitement at the chaos that was only the beginning.

Far away, across the waters, in a land that was hot, dry and barren. A rogue nation had decided they were tired of a world that wasn't fair. This time, they worked together to demand and get the respect they felt they deserved. Secretly they purchased the technology they would need so that they could let the world know who they were. They wanted to make certain that the world would never forget who they were and what they had accomplished.

Four men in white lab coats and protective face gear watched from a dry well beneath the arid desert. Inside what appeared to be a laboratory, to the left of a small rectangular window was a smaller still rectangle shaped box that was a timer. It was audibly counting down – twenty-five, twenty-four, and twenty-three. Reflecting from within the window, a massive light that illuminated the entire window commanded that the men look on. A closer look revealed an object.

It was long, round and spewing enormous amounts of combustion vapor through what appeared to be a tail. A two-toned red colored rocket popped up as the timer numbers diminished. Slim, with a large black cone-shaped tip, it began to shake. Soon it was as if it was going to burst from its seams. The timer blinked three, two, and one. The rocket launched as planned, as a circle appeared, exposing the rocket's head. Soon, there was more than merely space between the pad and the rocket. It had accelerated rapidly.

On the other side of the world, other countries were scrambling. All of the governments were contemplating the meaning of such a launch. Could it be what they feared most? Was it a launch with catastrophic proportions? In the US, at the white house, men dressed in black suits feared danger. In a Virginian white-stoned building, men and women scrambled to find answers, talking on their phones while cars were squealing past security gates.

Nations moved quickly to secure borders and provide air protection. Preparations for shooting down this rocket are under way. Countdowns were set in motion all over the world preparing a defense against the rogue country's rocket. News stations moved quickly to report the latest breaking news. Pictures of the rocket speeding through the space as it climbed to its unknown destination flashed across television screens. Seconds later the monitor would flash "Breaking News" that would interrupt local television programs. "A US submarine is under attack!"

The incident as it finally played out was only a routine patrol conducted by the submarine. Off the Alaskan coast, a Russian submarine appeared. The crew in the US submarine had identified the other sub as Russian. The Russian craft had opened its torpedo doors. The US crew then scrambled in preparation for an attack. A crew member on the ship shouted out,

"We're under attack! They are firing their weapons!"

The captain in charge immediately bellowed, "Man your battle stations! Prepare for attack!"

All that was occurring was surprising. The US submarine was preparing for battle against the unexpected. The communication between the two crews had been benign, just the day before. In the Pentagon, an official dressed in a sharp blue military uniform draped in numerous colored medals had asked his aide the obvious.

"What the hell is going on? Is this the end of the world?"

Rage was pleased with this turn of events, even though, in reality, he had little to do with the project. Destruction was like an aphrodisiac to him.

Meanwhile, at an elementary school in a small town in the Midwest the day began as any other. This particular school had built an enviable reputation for its ability to provide a great education. There were numerous awards displayed, given as rewards, over the last three years that echoed that sentiment.

Students filled the playground with squeals of laughter and joy. The happy sounds echoed off the building. There was a fight between two third grade boys. They occasionally break out on any playground. The taller boy, dressed in his blue school uniform, had a look of sheer hatred that was directed at the other lad who was smaller and wearing a slightly tattered uniform. The smaller boy looked sad. He had reached into his pocket and pulled out a weapon. He pointed it at the bigger boy.

A thirty-year-old schoolteacher fearing for her own and the children's safety had slowly walked toward the boy holding the weapon. She stood next to him.

"Damian, please give me the gun," she said softly, calmly, with a look on her face that telegraphed her desperation.

Damian hadn't given her the pistol. He had turned the shaking weapon toward her. He actually had a look of sheer fright. Other children screamed in panic. They ran. Students, along with their teachers scurried for cover. The staff still inside the school building wasn't aware of what was transpiring on the playground. Emergency preparation would be utilized today. They bolted out the door to help corral the kids once it became apparent that there was a real emergency. From her desk, the school secretary had immediately dialed 911.

"He cheated! He has to pay!," shouted an angry Damian.

"We will make certain that Roger, stays after school, Damian. Just give me the gun. It's going to be okay!" pleads the beleaguered teacher, Mrs. Smith.

She sensed that Damian might have given her the gun, and given the urgency of the situation, she decided to take a step forward, to put herself between Damian and Roger.

"No you won't. I will make sure he pays. I know all adults lie," claims Damian.

A shot rang out.

It had caused a wave of shock that virtually rippled the air across the playground. The whole scene was as if it had been choreographed especially for Rage's enjoyment.

"Start 'em young," he crowed. He was bent over with laughter. He reveled in the pain and confusion that were becoming a more and more familiar sight.

-3-

Appearing from the dust of the cosmos, a cloaked Llean-gellia hovered silently over the west coast. She viewed the scene in the two-story brick Victorian house. She realized that balance no longer existed. With urgency in her movement, she transformed into a shape that allowed her to reach Almightanius, who often appeared as a white orb. It took mere seconds for her to reach the kingdom of peace, joy and serenity. Immediately upon her arrival, Almightanius called to her, somehow sensing the burning energy that all but enveloped her. Without a word, Almightanius read her concern and immediately knew what had caused her to be ill at ease. *"I wanted her to tell me in her own words,"* thought Almightanius to himself as Lleangellia swooped quietly to a place in front of Almightanius.

She wasted no time with small talk, "Something has to be done. Somehow, 'evil' has gained more than just control. It has power over humans. Evil seems to be easy for those that come under its spell. There is never a backward glance, once a deed had been done. Things are out of hand. I am frightened."

Curious, Almightanius had asked, "What did you see?"

"A young man went to a website with a picture of the evil one etched into the background. After the young man logged off the computer, he looked as if he exploded. I saw an angry man kill his wife and his two children. There was more. In an unprovoked challenge, a Russian submarine faced off with an American sub. Another situation arose when Michelle, a sweet and beautiful woman, walked home and was attacked by three men in the park where many others walked by, never even lifting a finger to dial 911 or to help her in any way.

Almightanius had thought, *"These happenings could not become the norm. The world must not be in balance now. I believe 'evil' has found a way of misusing the humans' new technology, their Internet."* Then he spoke.

"Something had breached the Internet and it was being used to erode the quality of life on Earthios. My old friend seems to be doing anything within his power to pull as many people as possible under his control. The essence of "evil" is already making an impact with control over just a few. Just look at the toll today. If it keeps up, a many people will be under his thumb." It was becoming clear to Almightanius now, "I know he thinks he finally has me. He thinks he has gained the upper hand."

"You must go back to Earthios and continue monitoring. I will call for you soon. I have an important assignment for you. Your participation will be essential to make this disruption all end," instructed Almightanius.

"Of course," she replied and that she would return to her post, hovering over the action, wherever it was.

Lleangellia departed and Almightanius evaporated into a swirl of clouds just as he always had. Everything hadn't been changed. The Etherials were still gliding through the multi-hued skyscape. The large cloud lingered for only a moment, and then it disappeared.

Norevilania, still focused on gaining more control heard a loud and almost thunderous voice calling from nearby. He was actually talking to himself.

"It is really all over now! We must keep it going," he said finally, talking with the demoniac, who continued his influence over the network. He stared into the screen of the computer.

Calling from a place far away from the home base of either one of them, not wanting to visit Norevilania's actual domain, Almightanius called out for him.

"Norevilania, your presence is requested!"

Norevilania disappeared from his throne taking on the shape of a fireball.

"What did you think you were doing? Did you think I wouldn't notice?" demanded Almightanius. A dialogue had begun.

"What are you talking about? I haven't done anything that you haven't allowed," replied Norevilania sarcastically.

"Don't play with me! You found a way into Earthios using the forbidden. You take advantage of that. You have so many other ways to increase your kingdom. Do you really want to destroy the world? Do you really think you're going to get me this way?" queried Almightanius.

"Of course not!" He had said with a sly smile, "I'm not trying to get you. Why would I do that? What have you done to me?" His tone was sardonic, with a hint of resentment that was reflected by the deepening red of the fireball. "You've been so supportive of me. Why should I question or doubt anything you do?"

Almightanius seemed to boom as he showed his irritation. It was a reaction to Norevilania's mockery, which was evidenced by the darkening of the clouds that were gathering overhead. "You don't scare me! You know that the only way things can return to normal again is for you to find the lost power," a sputtering Norevilania had brought out. "If you look too hard, then everyone will know. You will lose respect." The cloud darkened all the more as Almightanius showed his anger, which was uncharacteristically tinged with embarrassment.

"Now you will need to change and do what you said you would never do, intervene within Earthios. You would use your powers to manipulate outcomes," Norevilania smirked. "Go ahead!" simpered Norevilania, growing tired of the exchange.

Almightanius thought, that Norevilania might have a point. *"Yes, he could use power to return the balance, but man would not understand. It would upset the flow that had insinuated itself into every facet of day-to-day life. Changes would mean that choice would be no more. Life on Earthios would not be as it was in the early years when man knew and understood that there were supernatural influences in the mix. That gift we had to take away. Man had understood the reasons. To introduce its return would create fear and uncertainty about who and what I represent. And those who lived in my kingdom or in Norevilania's would not be able to comprehend changes like that. I am sure the status quo must remain."*

Unfortunately he has a slight advantage just now. Balance will be restored though. He had sensed the possibility of real change, and it had caused a sly smile to appear. Remembering where he was, Almightanius brought his attention back to his foil.

"What do you think you'll gain from this, or should I say hope to gain?"

"Hmm, let me see. Well, how about you giving back my place in the kingdom for starters?" Norevilania threw back in an affected swishy voice.

"You know that's not happening," Almightanius said with a disgusted sigh.

Norevilania nearly spat out his reply, "I really don't need anything else, except maybe our trading places, since you won't allow me to return to the kingdom. How would you like to experience living in my kingdom?"

"Why do you ask for the impossible? You know that you won't be positioned to change everything that's been created," Almightanius said that, purely for clarity. There would be parameters.

Never one to like being outdone, Norevilania ended the discussion, saying, "I will return to my kingdom and continue." Quickly, in the span of a second, Norevilania's stopped his retreat

"A compromise might be in order. You've said what you wanted to say. Is there nothing else to be considered?" Almightanius spoke as if he were speaking to the open space. It was almost as if he already knew the answer.

"No. It is either back into the kingdom, or we do a trade. Nothing else will do!" Norevilania resolutely replied.

Reluctantly, after a lull in the conversation, he was certain both of them had much to think about. "Let humans decide" Almightanius had offered. "I can not agree to either of those requests, but if such requests can be considered by other means, Almightanius' was thinking aloud, "What are we to expect from allowing them make decisions that will most certainly mean change? The fact is, we both have a responsibility to our humans. We must decide whether we will "use" them in a battle where the consequence of losing –or winning, too– could change everything. We will engage in a battle for which the outcome would give you what you request, or you will return to your kingdom never to use any means to gain control over man. If you agree, we can talk in depth."

Norevilania wasted little time after the offer was proposed. He responded simply, "I'm listening."

"Okay. You must disconnect now. Stop your control over man until the battle is done. In other words discontinue using your machine. We each then agree to use one of our servants along with three humans for the battle. Your goal, as you stated would be to return to the kingdom. My goal would be to restore balance. Neither of us could use powers to influence or help the humans. Our servants would choose the three who will compete. The humans would have to volunteer to join the team. Agreeing would send the humans to another world where the battle would take place. Our servants won't use their abilities to manipulate outcomes. Humans will be able to use all resources. It will be teamwork at its best. Team members will be able to showcase their own special talents and utilize what they find in the new/other world. The battle will last seven days and will be considered won when at least two humans from the same team simultaneously utter or even think the words "surrender" or of course if they die," Almightanius plans aloud. –Norevilania thinks that there must be a trick involved, but is silent.– To make himself perfectly clear, Almightanius, –sensing Norevilania's misgivings– continued, "No tricks. You must remember that neither lying, nor trickery is within me."

Almost too quickly Norevilania piped in, "Okay, but with an addition. Each team has individual weapons. But, there is a more powerful weapon that must be set aside for each team to discover that could help them win the battle."

A nod of Almightanius' head sealed the agreement.

"Okay, deal it is!" Norevilania proclaimed.

A loud bang rang out. It signified that the deal had been sealed. They soon disappeared and made their way to their respective kingdoms.

Lleangellia was summoned on Almightanius' return. She was at the throne almost instantly.

"Things are different," began his lament. "I need you to guide a team of humans. I can't use my powers and you can't utilize your skills. It will be crucial to find a team of humans that will work together. They should have skills that will cover a variety of areas. They need good communication skills, be able to trust, have faith in others, be skilled in battle, but possess patience. All of these qualities should be familiar to you, because they are essentially what I requested of all of you in the beginning of our relationship. Norevilania will be in charge of the other team. I assume he will look for the antithesis of your choices. Most of all, his choices most certainly will be trying to demolish and dismantle our team. Our team must be strong. They should be able to withstand advances by the other team. A key attribute for team members must be "willpower". Of course it can be a man or a woman and they must be older than twenty. Wisdom and maturity is crucial. They will be provided with the best weapons at our disposal. I know that Norevilania will equip his team with a weapon that he feels will be defeat for our lineup. One of your responsibilities will be to lead the team to the shield that repels any weapon from Norevilania's crew. I've rambled on with my thoughts. Do you have any ideas?"

Lleangellia paused, "No, my Lord. Just give me some thoughts on where I should look to find the team."

"If we lose, –and I believe we won't–, you should know that Norevilania could potentially return to this kingdom. It cannot be allowed," Almightanius instructed.

"In forming our team, we must search everywhere. Your first stop will be Swedonia. I gave these humans additional genes of beauty. The criterion is simple. Utilize natural resources. The truth is of the most import. The chosen one should be able to make the choice of her/his own volition. When that choice has been solidified, then I will give you the next destination. Remember, I will know when the human accepts the challenge. I don't expect refusals, but choice should be an option. It is important. If that's clear, head to Swedonia, now."

Far away, in a dark, hot and frightening kingdom, another discussion was in the works. It was Norevilania and his prized demoniac, Rage. Soon after his arrival Norevilania had called for the demoniac.

"Rage, I need you now," he had ordered. Rage was soon beside the throne.

"We have a chance to return to the kingdom. Nothing should prevent us from getting back there. You must listen well! You must go out and find three miserable humans. Get the best of the worst. I only want those who excel at deception. They need to have the most evil, deceitful, cunning sort of character. But, they must be convincing. I want them to use every tool they have cultivated with their treachery. And they need to know how to fight. They must be the most beautiful men and women on the planet. The agreement is for three humans," Norevilania almost chokes out through the demon fire in his throat, but continues, "Unfortunately we are not supposed to use any of our power to influence the battle. They, too, will be armed with the best weapons available to them."

"Nominees are supposed to have a choice but we will offer them the world. It will be a choice they cannot refuse. The plan is to give up our portal. We will choose three humans as our representatives. They will go to an outer planet for the battle. It is over when two team members say or even imagine 'surrender' or of course if they are killed. An asset should be something that I made a part of the deal. You must make certain that our team finds the red sword. It will defeat any weapon the other team has. I am sure Almightanius has already sent his servant on the quest, so disconnect from the Internet and head for Earthios.

"First of all, I want you to go to Greeceia. The sexiest humans seem to live there. Are there questions?"

Rage had immediately shaken his head from side to side. He left and quickly disconnected from the Internet. Norevilania returned to the throne, sporting a visible sly smile.

-4-

She was sliding effortlessly over the pearl green water framed by tall, majestic mountains. Lleangellia cruised above it all, moving toward the beautiful brown sandy islands know as Sedona. That was the place. People living there had astonishing "godlike" beauty. The exotic dreamland's inhabitants lived their lives, making certain to keep their amazing physiques. On that sunny day men and women covered the sandy beach, basking in the sun. The end goal was to have a tan. It would mean their skin was the perfect color and the perfect texture. It was a day of indulgence. The beach bums were unaware of the enormous war that was about to begin. That day, they relaxed unknowingly relishing their oblivion.

An unlikely and unassuming fellow lived in that paradise. He was six feet two inches tall, and weighed in at a whopping two hundred-fifty pounds. He looked to be solid muscle. There was no paunch; no spare tire. He was solid and utterly fit. He had short black hair and a slight beard. This wasn't his native land. He had relocated to spend time preparing for his next show, to be staged there. He was an avid bodybuilder. He'd heard that this was the place to train. Having traveled all the way from the west, after winning a few small titles, it was time for what he called, "the big time". It was the serious stage; the big leagues. It was to be his next challenge.

Combining bodybuilding with martial arts was the latest kind of entertainment/competition. It required the ultimate training. He had realized that it was time to take his training to the top. Jesse had spent a lot of time on both bodybuilding and martial arts. He was in the best of both worlds now. His determination, power and unwavering focus would be optimum preparation for the most grueling training he would ever know.

Jesse sat on the patio of his comfortable, yet luxurious two-story old-fashioned, but upscale condominium. He was working on his laptop. He had been dating the same woman for a year and was sending an e-mail to his girlfriend when a knock came at his door. Initially, Jesse paused and turned toward the patio door not sure if he had actually heard the knock. Waiting a few seconds, he resumed working at his laptop. To himself, he said, "I need to finish this e-mail so I can get to the gym."

Another knock permeated the quiet. He ceased typing and called toward the door.

"Is someone there?" He clicked the icon that sent the message. He rose and headed toward the front door.

He muttered as he strode through the house, "Who could this be?"

He knew most of his friends were at work, or they were at the beach. He was a little anxious, but as always, prepared to deal with most anything. He looked through the peephole but there was no one there. Angry at the annoyance, he shouted to the unseen interloper.

"Hey! Is someone playing a game? Is it a neighbor kid? Is it a trick?" That said, he peered through the peephole. No one was in the door's see-through bubble's viewing path.

He turned back toward the patio and then he heard another knock. His frustration level began to rise as he approached the front door. Still nothing was visible through the peephole. He opened the door, ready to catch a menace. With the door open just wide enough, he stepped onto the walkway. Swiftly, he looked right, and then left, then toward the condo entrance. He became wary because he hadn't seen a soul. Then, at his left he noticed a neighbor couple leaving their unit. They responded to his glance, and the man nodded his head, acknowledging Jesse. Jesse nodded back and returned to his condo. He closed the door and turned, never expecting what would come next.

His eyes connected with an overwhelming figure that was standing in his living room. The figure was six foot five and slender. He was wearing a bright silk robe that was adorned with wide ridges at the collar and hem of the elongated robe. Jesse had frozen in his tracks, feeling as if he were trapped in a foot thick solid block of ice. He was unable to speak or move. He was staring as if he had seen a spectre or maybe it was an old-fashioned ghost.

26

Lleangellia recognized the fear etched on Jesse's face and she attempted to assure him by speaking in a soothing, soft, but commanding voice.

"No need to fear me. You are in no danger. You are safe."

Jesse was in shock, with only his head able to shed the sense of being part of an ice cube. He nodded to Lleangellia, acknowledging her statement. She nicely nudged Jesse toward a chair that was in the corner of the cozy living room. He was frightened. He was not sure just what was happening. He walked over to the smooth black leather lounge chair. He never took his eyes from Lleangellia's angelic presence. He was trancelike. The chair required both of his hands to allow his body to slowly sink into the familiar seat. He didn't need to look away. It was as if an unseen usher was guiding him. He sat up straight, because he couldn't relax. He listened.

"My name is Lleangellia," she began softly. –Jesse was paying attention, wide-eyed.– "I am from a land far away. It is a place where life here ends and another begins. Living there is complete peace and harmony. There are no troubles, no cares, and no worries about human frailties. Everyone's body is perfect in every way."

Curiosity was overtaking the silent trance. Jesse slowly muttered almost to himself, "What or who are you? Where is this place you speaks of?"

She heard the mutterings, and offered answers to the queries. She assured Jesse that she had answers to any of his questions. First, she offered an informative overview of Jesse's new reality. She felt his curiosity and hurried to let him in on the reason behind her visit.

"You are being chosen for an extremely important challenge. This challenge has requirements that you possess. You must be aware that there is no one with your blend of talents on Earthios."

"*What is she talking about – a challenge? Am I in trouble?*" Jesse was thinking when Lleangellia interrupted him.

"You are in no danger. It's just that your skills are exactly what will be needed to perform an heroic task that will keep the world, as we know it, from coming to an end. You have learned about good and evil. There is truth in most everything." –Jesse was now sitting on the edge of the chair. His trance was dissipating as his hearing became more focused.–

"Evil has always wanted to take revenge on the creator of your world," she continued, then paused knowing that Jesse would have questions. He did.

She began a well-worn narrative. "Almightanius is the one who created your world. There is a dark evil known as Norevilania. He disobeyed the only ancient law of truth and was banished from our world eternally. We must stop him again, now that he has found a way to spread his evil in this world. Almightanius could stop him, but your world would forfeit the precious gift of choice. Norevilania decided that he would make certain that the world pays the price for his banishment. Ultimately, it would be the end. He has begun already. He forces people to do things they would normally abhor. He makes them do evil. Will you help? You won't be alone. I will be there to guide you and two others through this war," pointed out Lleangellia.

Jesse just stared at Lleangellia once again in a trance. He had incredible difficulty comprehending what she had been saying. Now, he assumed that she was asking for help in saving his world. *"Is she asking me to help stop the world from ending? Do I say yes? It would be selfish to say no, but what would I get from this? Will I get to paradise? Will my wildest dreams be fulfilled?"*

Lleangellia immediately responded to his unspoken queries, "You will never want for a thing while you live on Earthios. You will have a place of comfort when your time there is finished." She knew his concerns, "Your friends and family, everyone, will only be saved when you help us defeat Norevilania."

Jesse bowed his head and shook it back and forth, not knowing what he should do. His right hand groped for his chin. He was thinking. *"This is unbelievable!"*

28

Lleangellia, gentle soul that she was, nearly offered support and encouragement, but she realized that he must make this choice of his own volition. She was remembering what Almightanius had told her. Time slowed and there were a few minutes with no conversation. Lleangellia was watching Jesse as he slowly raised his head toward her ethereal, expressionless face. He sighed, "Yes."

Lleangellia realized that it had been difficult for him. She was brief, "Jesse, you have made the right choice. You will never regret it. Remember, you are not alone. In a day or two I will return to prepare you and the others for the battle to come. Tell no one of this meeting. If you do, they will not believe you. It would be a waste of time. Remain here. Continue your training. I will call when it is time.

You will be brought to a place with the others and I will prepare all of you for the challenges you may face."

There were a few more details, but once outside, Lleangellia disappeared in a cloud of smoky vapor that was soon dissipated by a strong wind. Jesse stood stunned by all that had just transpired. He got up and began pacing from the kitchen to the living room. He looked down and touched the spot where Lleangellia had hovered. He occasionally would look for traces of her on the gold carpet. There was nothing to be seen but the tightly woven carpet fibers.

Questions and concerns swarmed in his brain. *Did I do the right thing? Will I survive? There isn't a choice. I must make sure my family and friends will live on. But then, is this Norevilania even real? Is there a connection? Has he done something that affected my friends or relatives?* He decided that he had better find the answers to those questions. He looked at the telephone. It was sitting on the wooden coffee table. But, in time, he remembered what Lleangellia said about telling anyone. Her glowing presence flashed through his memory.

"I will call my girlfriend and make sure she's okay though," he said to himself. He had dialed her number and soon there had been a, "Hello?" in a soft articulate feminine voice that nearly purred through the telephone line.

-5-

Norevilania's chief demoniac, Rage, was soaring amongst the stars. He was headed for the place where he knew he would find a team that would win the war. It was Greeceia. He was sure that he would soon find the first of his perfect team. He eyed an island and made straight for it. Illapogos was known as the island of perfection – men, women, children, too. He entered Earthios' atmosphere. His muscular frame disappeared, blending perfectly with the wind. He picked up speed quickly as he whizzed through the sky, approaching his target. No one noticed.

It was then that the demoniac decided on his landing tactics. Rage put down near where Miles was sunbathing. His skin was warm from the sun. Miles felt the urge to cool off, He moved toward the water's edge. The plan was to jump in the cool water and refresh his body. It had grown warmer from the time he had spent in the sun. Heads turned as he strolled past the numerous topless women and bikini wearing men. He stood six foot three and was solidly built at two hundred twenty-five pounds. His chin was square and he had chiseled features that went perfectly with his broad chest. He was sitting on the beach, enjoying the sun's rays. His skin was turning a perfect golden brown. Women and men walked past his reclining body. Personal focal points changed. His aura was magnetic. It was almost distracting.

Miles was a man that others admired. He possessed incredible intelligence, an amazingly perfect physique, a face that women swooned over, wit that could make even the quickest man or woman shudder, and it was topped off by a calmness that couldn't be shaken; even by the strongest earthquake. After reaching the edge of the water, he had stopped unexpectedly; mesmerized. The cool water began to cover his feet.

There in front of him, slowly rising from the water was an incredibly, stunning woman. She pulled her hair back from her face, to reveal smooth, tanned skin that was covering a perfectly shaped head, equipped with striking, sparkling blue eyes. He looked around to see if anyone else noticed this treasure. Scanning the right and left side of the beach, no one had looked in his direction. He shook his head as if to waken from a dream. Soon after gazing at this beautiful woman, he immediately thought he was falling in love. *"I have never seen anyone so gorgeous,"* he thought to himself.

She noticed his interest, and stopped about five feet in front of him. She shyly eyed him, encouraging him to join her. Unable to resist her advances, and now wearing a huge smile, he had walked slowly into the water to meet her.

"I could be in love! I am so unbelievably lucky," he had whispered aloud as he approached her. Her smile continued. It was apparent that her nearness was influencing his actions.

"How are you?" she asked as she was bending toward him.

She was exciting to look at. He noticed that one of her perky breasts was positioned just above the shimmering surface of the water. Her beauty mesmerized Miles. He was nearly glassy-eyed but he could still think. He wondered what she wanted. It only needed her to ask. After a time, he realized she was speaking to him,

"What is you name?"

The reply, of course, was, "Miles, and yours?"

She seemed to be moving closer, her breasts in the lead, "Princess."

By then, Miles realized that there was an overwhelming yearning creeping into his core. He was considering the possibility of being intimate with her. Princess knew. She continued her erotic advances. Her spell seemed to go unnoticed by him. It wasn't long before she knew he wouldn't provide a roadblock to any of her advances.

"Do you live nearby?" she asked not so innocently.

Miles found a bit of aplomb somewhere under the confusion that enveloped the moment, "Not too far from here, actually."

She purred when she responded, "I don't know this area. It would be wonderful to have someone show me around."

Miles seemed to slip into a more familiar mode of behavior after processing the request.

"I'll show you a good time. Oops, I meant to say 'round.'" There was a bit of embarrassment at that slip of the tongue.

She feigned a sad expression and said, "That would be great. I hope I'm not inconveniencing you. I mean, you probably have a woman in your life."

Almost too eagerly he offered, "No – single."

Miles was smiling broadly and she grinned back. Both of them were expertly treading water, and it made them softly bob up and down, setting a tempo for their chatter. They moved further and further from the shore. It now seemed as if they were the only ones in the water. Miles felt his libido add some intensity, but he was distracted by everything about her – the sweet soft voice and her dazzling beauty were only starters.

"Is there a place where we might have food? All this swimming has made me thirsty, too," she asks.

Miles points up the hill, "My place is there, and I have pretty much anything that could satisfy a thirst. We could be there in minutes, and we don't have to drive."

She waited to respond to set the scene, "Okay."

Princess planted her feet on the floor of the sea and rose to expose the voluptuous figure that had been hiding under the surface. Watching her materialize for the first time, Miles had to stifle a nearly audible gasp that made his entire being smolder with desire. Princess then walked from the water, closely followed by Miles. Her stride was exaggerated for his benefit. Heads turn as they passed others. Miles noticed the warmth creeping into his loins and he looked for a distraction. Too much information was not a good thing right now. It hadn't taken long to reach the place where the golden sand began to dust the black cobbled road that led north, toward town.

Walking leisurely, they passed stone colored condominiums. It's still a quarter-mile to Miles' place. Bicycles and small energy efficient cars were frequenting the one-lane road. He was unable to tear his gaze from Princess though. Miles nearly tripped on a small stone.

Princess was asking him why he hadn't a special person in his life while she fiddled with her hair. She did it a lot. She took her right hand and gracefully tucked the wayward lock of hair behind her ear.

"I mean everything – work, pleasure, whatever,"she purred

Miles was used to answering questions. He responded quickly.

"I am an accountant. I have my own firm. As for pleasure, I love to treat and care for lovely people, such as you, and I like to rest in the sunshine, on the beach. How do you get by?"

Princess answered furtively, "I like to travel all over the universe. I mean world." –Rage was irritated by this slip and vowed that he would be more careful.– Quickly moving on, she said, "Actually, beside that, I don't do much. I like to make certain that people get what they want out of life. Do you have what you want?"

Miles pondered, rubbing his square chin with his left hand, "Hmmm. The only thing I can think of would be to have a special someone in my life. It seems as if everything is about where it should be."

They were still strolling toward his sheltered little villa, and heads were still following the pair as they made the turn to enter the complex. It was small and cozy, with only four cottage style condos in the compound.

He was still thinking aloud, "It all depends, but if it meant that I could spend time with you, it sounds as if it could be a worthwhile endeavor."

Princess felt his interest and played along. She batted her eyes at him and smiled coyly, saying, "Who knows what could be possible. Play your cards right and…"

It seemed as if this was the perfect opening for Princess to try a bit of her kind of honesty.

"I have a problem that you may be able to help solve. I need your help with something extremely important," she earnestly set forth. She watched Miles' face and saw that he was concerned.

"What is it?" he replied immediately.

They were inside the condo soon, and as they entered the incredibly beautiful structure that had a contemporary and fashionable feel to it they chatted. It was an incredible room. Each piece of furniture had a natural shape and the earthy colors gave it a gentle aura. Miles and Princess were so engrossed; so engaged in their conversation that they sat in unison, side-by-side on the beige curvilinear loveseat.

Miles was genuinely worried. He faced Princess and she was the focal point of his attention. His mind was working like a well-oiled machine. –Her thoughts were directional. The deal was sealed; she knew her task was accomplished.–

Her face was masked from much practice. She took a breath, and with a sad expression that had worked before.

"There is a "person" if he can be referred to as that, who has been trying for as long as I can remember, to prevent me from seeking fulfillment. I need to help others, so they can live a more complete life. It is in my heart." She paused for effect, her face carrying a look of concern and urgency. She went on, "He is working to make it all stop. It will be a reality unless I can get someone to take away the source of his abilities. His company needs to be destroyed."

Miles was anxious and worried. He was thrilled to be with her, but he couldn't ask more questions. It was confusing and wonderful all at the same time. He could only utter, "What can I do?"

She began reciting her well thought out strategy, "I need to have you work as part of a team that I'm assembling. My oppressor needs to be brought to his knees and then obliterated. It is the only plan that has a chance. It must be implemented."

He was quick on the pickup, "Whatever you need, I'm in."

Princess gave the impression that she was genuinely appreciative, "Thank you so much."

Miles leaned toward Princess, who offered a warm hug. It was returned in kind, and the heat of her body was like an elixir to him. It fueled Miles' aroused imagination, and he thought of nothing more than lying next to her, naked, in his bed. His luck wasn't changing much, though.

34

Princess pulled away from him, wearing a sad expression, "I have to go. I have to prepare. I will be back in a day or two. When I return, we will spend time together. I will look forward to that time."

He wasn't quite sure what it meant, but he begged to come along. He was offering whatever she needed. She would have none of it. It didn't fit her plan of action.

She was almost out the door when she said, "No, there isn't a thing you can do right now. I will return. I promise then that we can spend time together. I hope that sounds good to you. It sounds wonderful to me."

All of that may have assuaged his concerns, because he acquiesced, "Okay. I will be ready for your return."

He was disappointed. But, he did believe that she would come again. She turned and walked toward the door, but returned and brushed her full lips against his. It had such an impact that Miles nearly crumpled to the floor when his knees turned to jelly. It was a slow kiss, and Miles sensed a future for the passion. It was spellbinding. As she moved through the door, she blew him a sweet kiss and closed it behind her. Almost before it clicked shut, he had the handle in his hand, pulling it open, hoping for a last glimpse and another goodbye kiss.

She had disappeared as if she were a ghost. He didn't believe his eyes and he looked back and forth, trying to catch sight of her. But, she was gone. Rage had been successful in acquiring his first team member. He soared into the lovely sunset and was patting himself on the back. "What a brilliant disguise!" snickered the nasty demoniac. He had no morals. He had no need for them. He was pure evil.

-6-

Lleangellia was soaring effortlessly through the sky, heading to the US. It was an area where winters are fierce and the summers are often dreary. Just as often, the heat was fierce. It was the time of year when the colors of the trees begin turning from green to a multitude of amazing orange and deep red hues. It was a good day. She continued to flutter above the town littered with brownstones.

She was looking for someone. Her quest was to seek a specific young woman who was small in stature, but huge in heart and faith. Her brunette hair was long and curly, and it cascaded past the middle of her back. She was well proportioned. But her best trait was that she was patient. –She was like a snake waiting for a meal; trying to get within striking distance of its prey; never waving from the prize in the end.– She had skills that could spin the most negative situation into something optimistic. She had faith that could drive a car a hundred miles on mere fumes.

April was five feet tall and weighed a very compact 100 pounds. That day, she was in the park, with a book. Sitting on a green metal-framed bench, facing the expansive lawn, listening to chirping birds. She was reading. It was a beautiful day. She was happy. Her day had begun as always, with a wholesome breakfast and then she had dutifully and happily meditated. She had even had time to take care of her houseplants. Everything in her world was copacetic.

Lleangellia had seen her "subject" sitting on the bench and the opportunity seemed perfect. Her arrival was silent, and she walked toward her reading target. The birds were chirping their utter excitement at the state of the weather, and a feathered friend was soon perched on her left shoulder. She stood ten feet from April, as the chirping birds finally caught April's attention. As April looked up, she noticed the angelic figure standing nearby and wondered if she was dreaming. The spectre was lovely, and she wondered if she was seeing things. There was a bird on her shoulder.

36

April was enthralled. She invited Lleangellia to join her on the bench. The anxious apparition instructed the bird to fly away, fearing it would be the focal point of any discussion that arose. That was not what she wanted.

While the two women were engrossed in their meeting, Rage was scanning the skies, preparing to head many miles away in the other direction. He traveled to a tropical island where the weather was almost always perfect. He was focused on another young woman.

She was barely five foot three, and she was meditating in her tiny bedroom. She was extremely fit. Because she had lost many family members in unthinkable tragedies, she had contempt for religion and had turned her focus inward, trying to cultivate an inner power. She had developed combat ninja-type skills for assurance. Since her mastery of those skills, no one had been better than she – not even a man. She was small, but strong. She could pack a wallop. Her name was Eun. As she sat on the floor, she thought there had been a soft knock at the door. Quietly, she listened, unsure if it was a knock or just a noise magnified by the stillness inside the flat.

The staccato repeated itself, but louder, "Knock, Knock." Eun jumped and forced her eyes to open slowly. She raised her head and began to unreel her body from her meditation pose. She was already in a defensive mind-set.

She walked slowly toward the door and as she moved, her stance became more aggressive. All that training had left an indelible mark on her psyche. She knew that no matter what was on the other side, she was up for it. Standing in front of the still closed door, she listened for breathing. She had demanded in a collected, calm, strong voice, "Who is it and what do you want?"

Meanwhile, at the park, April asked spoke with Lleangellia.

"Would they come to me?"

"I think animals come to those who have an aura of peace and harmony about them."

It made sense to April.

Lleangellia explained that the bird's name was Eve and then she said that she would try to call her now. The blue jay was singing in a nearby tree and Lleangellia crooned to her, reaching out with her right hand, "Eve, come to me."

The bird gave April a once over and slid off the branch flapping toward the sky, not in their direction. She came back through, coming close to them, but it was a tease. She swooped higher and circled three or four times, keeping her distance. The third circuit completed her preparation and she slowly moved out of the skies toward the park bench and after another go-round, landed on April's left shoulder. April was relaxed and Eve seemed comfortable, sitting on April's shoulder verifying her presence with a chirpy song. It was the perfect set-up for Lleangellia. She knew it was time. Launching into her plea without a preamble, she asked, "Would you be willing to help me? Earthios is in danger of being destroyed. Many want to see it obliterated."

Enchanted by the presence of Eve, April was distracted and didn't grasp completely what Lleangellia was asking. Before she could sort through the confusing moment, she inexplicably, but enthusiastically said, "Yes!"

To Lleangellia, the deal was sealed. Lleangellia didn't give it another thought; she wanted to move on with her search for the final member of the team.

"I will be back to give you more detail and provide you with all that you will need. Eve will stay with you until I return." She continued with an aside to the little blue bird, "Take care of her, Eve."

There was a return chirp from Eve and Lleangellia moved away, leaving April engrossed with Eve. April rose up with Eve still on her shoulder and walked north out of the park, as she always had. The only difference was that today, Eve was there.

Relaxation was a constant companion for Eun. She did what she normally did. She meditated. Today, there had been a knock at the door and Eun thought she was prepared for what was on the other side. Rage, the demoniac who had been appointed Lleangellia's opponent, was there. From the other side of the door, he sensed her apprehension and called out, "I am not here to harm you."

The usually cautious Eun decided that it was safe to open the door, then pulled back, "Wait a minute," she thought, *"Why am I allowing access to my home to a stranger?"*

Rage knew that he must present a benign façade to put her at ease. He decided on Rachael, a middle-aged woman who was asking for help. The ruse worked and Eun backed away from the door and slowly grasped the round doorknob with her left hand. She moved it to the left and soon the open door revealed a small figure.

It was a slightly grey-haired woman who looked as if she was someone's grandmother. She appeared frail and was waiting for a response. Eun motioned for her to enter. The woman slowly walked past her, into the dimly lit room, talking, as she walked. Eun closed the door and followed along behind her, taking in the unfolding scene. The visitor launched into a narrative.

"My name is Rachael. I live on the island. I was born here – always lived here. I try to keep to myself, never hurt or bother anyone. A short time ago, someone took my identity. Now, I am on the verge of losing all that I have – my home, my savings – things that I have worked hard for. I need your help to get it back. I heard from a close friend that you could take care of such things, but in a quiet way. I can pay. Please help me."

Warily, Eun asked, "What is it that you want me to do?"

Rachael smiled a crooked little smile, and offered, "Make them sorry for what they did. I want you to do what you do best."

Eun knew that the woman wasn't likely going to accept a "no" answer. Empathy began to creep into every pore of Eun's being. She had taken in Rachel's torn and tattered appearance and now she was beginning to seethe. Someone had stolen this woman's life. This poor defenseless woman had been wronged.

She gave an emphatic go ahead to Rachael. Asking for details that were promised when the woman had said she needed to be certain of a few details.

"Thank you for doing this. Now, I can have my life back. I didn't deserve this," the disguised demoniac skillfully whined, "I will return tomorrow." She immediately turned toward the front door, opened it and just as quickly closed it behind her.

Eun stood still, unsure of what had just played out. She turned around, bowed her head and began her meditation anew. All the while, knowing that she would have to exterminate someone very soon.

-7-

Tomorrow would come soon enough for Eun. The sun was actually setting on the island, but it was rising in the east. Lleangellia had been gliding through the horizon silently. No one but Rage noticed. They had exchanged animosities as they wove through the atmosphere. Rage used his arm in an attempt to strike fear into Lleangellia. It hadn't worked. Lleangellia had smiled back at Rage. Intent on the task at hand, it made him mutter with a snarl, "She's going down!"

The land below Lleangellia was serene. It was dry and sandy. There were people moving determinedly across the desert. Some camped in tents and others were pulling their camels along behind them. She continued forward, finally seeing buildings and no more tents nor square buildings that had been the usual just minutes ago. It looked like a big city.

Lleangellia walked down the road leading to the center of town. There were high-rise buildings surrounding the city center. It looked as if the stained glass in the windows were framing for the outside of the edifice. Looking up, she walked down the grey cement walkway. There were numerous women and men stepping quickly. They all had something to do. Their sheer numbers could have been an advertisement for diversity. Young, old, big, small, it was a virtual variety pack. The dress code was very interesting to the unnoticed observer who had a fashion sense of her own.

Many of the women were using cream-colored face shawls. There was a story behind it. In their culture, many women didn't feel comfortable showing their face. –Those struggling with feminism issues didn't cover their faces; publically protesting the days of covering women's faces should be over.–

The walk took Lleangellia about three blocks to a high-rise building. Gold colored brick distinguished it from the others nearby. The pinnacle of the structure was cone shaped, with antennas protruding from it here and there. Facing the building, she tried to gaze toward the twenty-third floor. *"He is there,"* she thought to herself as she moved toward the entrance. It was ten feet of glass doors that defined the entryway itself. Square gold-plated door handles open the doors. She walked through the first glass doors. With a few steps, she began her entry into the second set of doors, moving into the grand vestibule area, which was replete with two security guards. Attendants were scanning monitors that insured the safety of the building.

It was customary for visitors to check in at the large marble topped, oval desk that was identified as the "Information Desk". Something on the floor distracted the attendant who was groping behind the counter, seeking a misplaced bit of paperwork. It was the perfect diversion. Lleangellia slipped by, unseen. The elevators were beckoning, even though she'd never seen one. She scanned the face of elevator wall and was thoroughly confused by the lack of information. A gentleman suited in grey was in a hurry and he pressed the red "Up" control. She took note of the procedure and followed the man into the elevator. He pushed fifteen, and she pressed twenty-three. The doors closed and the elevator moved up. Watching the oaken doors close, smiling to herself, Lleangellia knew she had learned something.

At the fifteenth floor, the elevator stopped. The doors opened and the man exited quickly, turning to his right. He walked quickly, and his shoes made sounds of a click, click, click that echoed down the hallway. The doors closed. She was happy to soon be face-to-face with her third choice. He was intelligent, an engineer.

He appeared to others a meek man. He was average in stature, yet his face was handsome. He often took on work for religious reasons. He was spiritual. This particular mission, actually an internship, had him working with locals to restore several sacred buildings in the vicinity. Wear, tear and corrosion, brought about by extreme weather had severely damaged several of the structures he was restoring.

Lleangellia reached the twenty-third floor. The door opened and she walked out of the elevator. The walls were cream-colored – Navajo white came to mind. There was a huge placard with names and office numbers listed in alphabetical order. Williams Engineering was in room 2305. Walking in that direction, she was nearly to the door when it opened and out walked a very nice looking young man. He was walking quickly, head down, engrossed in thought. Noticing the beautiful woman, dressed in white trimmed in gold, stopped him in his tracks though. The woman looked ethereal to him. It was almost as if she was a vision, born in his dreams. She wanted him to perceive her as a friendly interruption.

"Do not be alarmed. You are in no danger. May I join you? I would like you to see something."

Jake was usually cautious, but it was as if he were inside a daydream. His head moved up and down, conveying both confusion and approval.

Jake followed Lleangellia who was asking, "How are you today?"

The small talk continued when Jake offered, "Good. Busy. The day is going well."

She followed up with, "Being busy can be a good thing. It keeps the mind from wandering to regrettable thoughts."

"It's been hard at times, but it makes you stronger," Jake suggests. The chatting is coming easier.

Lleangellia pipes in with, "You're right." The chitchat continued.

Still conversing, they walked toward one of the glass balconies that faced three pyramids in the distance. They reached the balcony, where Lleangellia was effusive as she gazed at the vista that seemed almost fanciful.

She cooed, "Isn't it amazing? It is beauty that man has created. It would be a shame for it to be destroyed."

Jake thought she was referring to an end that wasn't orchestrated by a mad man, and he offered, "Well, it's going to be decimated in the end anyway."

Quickly, Lleangellia almost shouted her reply, "I'm talking about before that end."

Now he showed concern, "What do you mean?"

She looked at him almost pleadingly and said, "There is a being that wants to destroy Earthios, and I need your help to insure his defeat."

His full attention was directed toward Lleangellia and he blurted out, "Anything to save the planet. I never want to see this beauty destroyed."

This was the response that Lleangellia had hoped for. She smiled and assured him, "You won't regret this decision. I will be back and give you details. You will know what you need to do."

She turned, leaving Jake to look over the balcony at the landscape he so loved. He lowered his head, closed his eyes and mused, to himself, *"I'm not sure what it is that I am in the middle of, but I believe that I have made the right decision. I really wonder why I was chosen. I will make certain that every ounce of my being can be used to fight this mad person. I need to make sure this planet survives."* Knowing that further mulling of the events of the past hour could mean only more confusion, he closed his eyes for a moment, raised his head and turned and walked back toward his office.

Lleangellia left the building and rushed straightaway for the sky. She had her team assembled and it was time to report to Almightanius. She was excited about what she had accomplished. Her team would bring balance back to the universe and end this terrible game.

Rage had picked up his pace to complete his team. He was more motivated after seeing the enemy, Lleangellia. Urgency was his focus now. His pursuit had led him to a city that was always host to tourists. It had one of the oldest and tallest buildings in the northern hemisphere. He found himself heading to the part of town with a history. Survival was the name of the game in that locale. His last team member choice was living in a seedy one-bedroom apartment there. He knew how to survive. He was young and tall. He was brawny and his short brown hair was cut close to his head. He was thirty, and he had a look. Of course, he was a loner. He knew many people, but they didn't know him.

He was Devon. Some of his abilities weren't laudable. He was a master of deception. He could use his wiles to fool the smartest and wisest. He had honed this skill over a long period of time, and he had used the Internet to augment this most dubious skill. Many a night he spent time on the Internet trying to mislead others. He always kept his true identity a secret in his wanderings there. The Internet was an amazing tool.

Devon was sitting in his sparsely furnished living room eating lunch. His hastily constructed ham and cheese sandwich were evidence of his hunger. His ample bites were making it disappear quickly. He was sitting on a worn metal chair with his laptop on the metal table that was stationed near the chair. There was music playing in the background. He was startled and stopped eating, turning his attention toward the door. *"Who the hell is that?"* he thought to himself. He turned and began maneuvering to extricate himself from the metal chair and table. He reached the door quietly and looked through the peephole. He saw darkness. He was intrigued and slowly cracked the door open, just enough to peek further than the peephole bubble encompassed. He decided then to pretend he was out. Quickly, it was apparent that plan wouldn't work. The trickster, Rage was whispering from the other side of the door.

"I have a gift for you. Let me in and we can talk."

Devon was who he was, and he wasn't sure yet about opening the door. He was interested, but he wasn't sure about unlatching it.

The voice on the other side was urgent, "Devon, trust me. It is worth your time."

All his life, he had wanted to be powerful, and Devon threw caution to the wind and opened the door. It revealed a tall figure dressed long black silk robe. He was mesmerized by an oddly impressive figure standing in the frame of his door.

Rage gave it no thought and strolled to the center of the room and proceeded to sit. Devon took a last peek out the door into the hallway and made sure no one was waiting in the hall. He closed the door and gazed at Rage.

"People are trying to take over the world and extinguish all that is wonderful. If you won't help, you will no longer have

45

the privacy that you have now. Everyone will know who you are and what you have done."

"If you help, I'll make certain that you are one of the most powerful beings on this planet," Rage intoned.

"Why me?" Devon wanted to know.

Rage quickly responded with what he knew Devon needed to hear, "Your intelligence, cunning, subtlety and the ability you have to stay anonymous will be important when the destroyers implement their line of attack. It will be easy to combine your skills with theirs and make this a snap."

Devon wanted to know whom he would be working with, and when he asked.

Rage was quick to say, "You know none of them; nor they you." The demoniac was looking to move along. He wanted his answer, and he wanted to leave. Being an intuitive sort, Devon knew there had to be more, but he wanted to be able to control minds.

"What do you want?" the demonic led with.

"I want the ability to control minds," Devon said smiling.

"I can give you that ability, but something better; the ability to read minds," Rage put forth.

Devon's face had lighted with astonished excitement when he responded, "Yeah, yeah. That is it. How do I know that you are going to follow through and really give me what I want? It could be a trick."

Rage had expected that, and offered, the tried and true, "Trust me."

Devon doesn't have a chance, because Rage can exert an unseen control over any situation, and he was quick to say, "Okay, I will do it." He is thinking of the minds that he could read.

Devon was still sitting when Rage left swiftly, promising to return in a short time with instructions. The door soon closed and Devon turned back to eating his sandwich. He was excited with the promises that Rage had given him, but he was still hungry. He was looking forward to the mission.

Rage had exited and disappeared in a flash. He returned to Norevilania's lair. As he traveled he thought about the three who would be part of his team. His roster was complete –

Devon, Eun and Miles. Each of them was uniquely positioned to be more powerful than Almightanius' crew. There was no

way he could even fathom dealing with a loss. He was looking to regain control, which would mean that he would never have to endure that wretched, hot place again.

Norevilania was on his throne as he welcomed Rage and regaled him with questions about their project.

"Well?" was all he said.

"I have assembled the team, your majesty. I think that of all the humans available, I have chosen the best for our purposes. We will not fail," Rage answered with enthusiasm fueled by adrenalin left over from his journey.

Norevilania looked thoughtful and began to speak, "I would imagine that Almightanius has gathered his team too. That means that I will be receiving a call soon. Please make certain they are provided with the most reliable weapons so that when they reach the planet scheduled for the battle, it will ensure victory. Almightanius didn't say that we couldn't take them with us. And who cares what we do, as long as we are victorious?"

Rage had been awaiting the question and said, "I have the weapons which I will carry with me. The red sword and the stick will be strategically placed so that they can be easily found." As an after thought, a part of his game plan was revealed when he added, "Miles will find the sword, Eun the stick, of course. How should we go about preparing the team?"

Accustomed to calling the shots, Norevilania began, "Gather the team and brief them. You will transport them to the country that is known for the animals and there they will be told what is expected of them and what will transpire. It is important to reiterate the rewards that are awaiting them, and often. It will keep them motivated. Of course, explain that they will be taken to another place where their opponents will be working to destroy them. They must understand that it is a fight to the death if no other outcome is possible. It is very important for them to be allowed questions. If there is an attempt to influence their participation, you know what to do."

Rage acknowledged Norevilania's instructions with a mere nod of his head.

In a more serene place that was far from Norevilania's throne, a different scene was unfolding. It was a meeting between Lleangellia and Almightanius. Urgency was in the air, but it had been tempered with civility.

Lleangellia smiled and bowed to show her respect, saying, "We have all of the participants. They have freely agreed to help us."

Almightanius didn't want to remind her, but he did, "I know." His easy manner sometimes caused others to forget the scope of his powers, "You did a great job. I knew I could count on you. But, this is where the faith enters the picture. We have the right people, but are we sure they can withstand the challenge and survive? On their own, they won't. We have to give them something that I promised I wouldn't. Norevilania has already broken the agreement just as I expected he would. We will help the team."

There was surprise on the countenance of Lleangellia who stifled a small gasp as he continued, "I know we promised no unnatural assistance, but it is a must right now. The assistance will be almost natural. I still want you to avoid using your power unless it is essentially the only option." Lleangellia nodded in understanding.

Almightanius kept speaking, "I didn't want to do this, but my hand was forced. They were given the ability to manipulate portions of the planet. Each of them will have personalized and unique abilities. They must not know that in the beginning. They will discover their augmented powers when they are in preparations for the battle. I know that trusting Norevilania was a mistake, but I hoped he'd keep his word. Actually, he kept part of it. He didn't use his influence on Earthios. Now, they need to know what is going to take place; where it happens and they must be aware of what could be in store for them. There is gravity to this situation that may be difficult to understand. They will need encouragement and reminders that their skills are extraordinary and that is why they were chosen to be a part of the team. Norevilania's team will be tricky and he will support them anyway that is possible. It's likely you already know all of this but I think reminders are often helpful. You will be challenged in ways that you may not remember going through before. Everything could be different, even the terrain. It will be important for the three to become familiar with what they will encounter. I won't be able to help. Your faith will be important. Remember always, that in essence I will be beside you, just a thought away. The victory will be ours. I will destroy Norevilania's ability to exert his influence on earth. He does not know now, but his reign is over. He will never regain his power," she declared while kneeling.

"Go now and prepare for battle. Afterward, you can return to the green pastures and the peaceful existence that you deserve. I will send another monitor to Earthios, unless you request that you continue as before."

Lleangellia had no intention of ever retiring, but acquiesced, "I would like to continue my job, but if you prefer that I retire, then that is my wish."

Almightanius spoke softly, but firmly, "I am offering you what I offered humans, choice. Because your commitment and faith is so strong, and I am very sure we will have a victory in this battle, you have eared the right to make that request. Of course you will be allowed to continue. But, now it is time. I will wait until after you have briefed your players to send Rage, his team and you and yours to the place where the battle will commence. The battle will be in seven human days and evil will surrender. It is a bit longer than I would have hoped for, but you have the information and please, know that if you have need for anything all you must do is ask. Following your briefings, the next stop will be to the setting for the battle."

Lleangellia had nodded in agreement. She was anxious and ready.

-8-

Lleangellia rose and took her leave. She retraced her route, heading back toward her very first destination. She saw the sandy beaches and was soon knocking on Jesse's door. It was midmorning and Jesse was about to leave for his early workout. He had been keeping his usual routine. Just as he zipped his gym bag, the knock came to the door. He opened it to a smiling Lleangellia. He bowed his head and invited her in.

She entered and said, "Come with me. I will explain everything when we meet the others."

Jesse reminded her of their earlier conversation, "I thought you would explain when you returned. Do I get to speak with my family?"

Calmly, Lleangellia reassured him, "Your family will be fine. I will make sure they are protected. Now you need to be ready to go. I know that it is confusing being on this roller coaster, but you will be fine. We must leave immediately. You will need to bring nothing along with you."

Jesse walked to the door and as he was reaching for the handle he looked back at his home, but it was only for a moment. In a flash, they had both disappeared. Jesse was transported ahead toward Almightanius' designated location. –The plan had been to have each of the team members arrive at the same time and this sent Lleangellia to fetch April.–

Jesse was traveling slowly or so it seemed. It was a mode of transportation that no human had experienced prior to then. His body almost felt as if it was seeping through a fabulous wormhole, all the while breaking rules of time and space. His body seemed to push through some kind of separation of the elements. He was aware of, but couldn't see nor hear the panorama of sounds that surrounded his journey.

It would have been too much for his brain to comprehend Jesse began to think, as he was being transported to wherever he was headed. His mind was forming complete thoughts though, *"This is amazing. There is something seriously incredible about this whole endeavor. Who will we be pitted against? Where will they come from? Are they odd appearing aliens or is this something that higher beings do for laughs? We all will have a lot to learn. Can we rise to a level where winning a competition is possible?"*

On the way to meet April, Lleangellia was thinking, something she often did when she was traveling, *"Etherials, to which I am similar, have a superior life form and incredible intelligence, traits that allow us to have the ability to withstand persuasion that could result in irreversible consequences that would mean banishment, were we to give in to the pressure. Humans, on the other hand, don't always seem to resist temptation. It could have been a real coup for humans to utilize their natural strengths in the battle that would come. Almightanius was going to win. There was too much at stake. They would be more powerful than any human ever imagined. I have faith, but I must admit, I am worried."* She quickly cursed herself.

"Shame on me. This is a moment of doubt that cannot exist. Forgive me, master."

The master heard and understood, "It's okay. It is only natural that your faith in humans may waver. Continue to have faith in what you do. Please know that I have faith in you and the decisions you may make." It was telepathy at its finest.

Lleangellia's thoughts weren't apt to deter her from the path toward April. She was meditating at home as usual. There was a tranquil blend of sounds coming from outside the window. It was Eve.

She provided a voice and a song that were perfect for meditation. April's eyes were closed and she was breathing softly. She was almost in a state of bliss. The moment was interrupted when Eve sang quite a few misplaced, but happy sounding notes. Eve had anticipated Lleangellia's arrival. April noticed a difference in the moment right away and begins to come out of her meditative state. Her breathing began to increase and her muscles awakened with the increase in the blood flow. Her eyes opened.

By the time the sound arrived, she was fully aware of a knock on the tall, heavy oaken front door.

The beach was overseeing the day's beginnings as it always had. The waves were lapping at the moist sand that was smoothed and waiting for sandpipers to leave their oddly forked footprints to welcome the new morning. Miles had gone to the shore with his usual gear, having left his small villa. There was no one around on the simply gorgeous, sunny morning.

He was walking on the grey colored stone road that led toward the sandy beach. It was glowing with golden hues in the morning light. He was startled by a tall figure standing in the pathway in front of him. A black and red robed spectre simply appeared. Miles responded a bit slower than his usual instantaneous reaction.

"Can I help you?"

Rage peeked from under the hooded robe.

"Princess needs your help. She begged me to come to you. She said you had been willing to help her when she spoke with you before, and now she is in dire need. Please come, now!"

Miles' head felt as if the individual hair shafts were receiving repeated electrical shocks when he said, "Who are you? Is she okay? Where are we going?"

The subterfuge was easy for Rage.

"I am Princess' aide. We are headed to meet her. She will tell you everything she needs when I have delivered you to her and you are safe."

Rage made a point of referring to Princess, to keep the make-believe Princess a reality for Miles. He knew that Miles was genuinely concerned about the incredibly beautiful woman who he wanted to remain in his life. Miles was usually cautious and thoughtful when he made decisions, but wasted no time agreeing to go with Rage, who just as quickly listed the "rules" for the journey.

"You will feel tingling in your stomach. Don't let it worry you. You will be fine. Just hold on to me. Do not let go," Rage called out as he motioned Miles to join him.

Rage and Miles disappeared. They were flying through the atmosphere, falling like a star streaking through the night sky. The droning sound that Miles heard wasn't just the whistling wind, it was Rage, who was relating need for speed.

Miles was anxious and he asked again and again, "Where are we going?"

It was obvious that Rage was frustrated with the inquiries when he shouted, "We are picking up the others. We are running out of time!" Miles was even more worried, "What is the trouble?" he said before he was silenced by Rage's response, "No more questions. I will explain when everyone is together. There is no need to keep asking the same questions over and over."

Their journey continued with much urgency. Miles was just behind Rage and the breezes in their face were strong. In just a few minutes, the blazing speed of their travel landed them on the isle of relaxation. Eun's door was in front of them. Rage said, "She is one of the two who will join us. Just stay behind me and I will talk. We will tell her briefly what is expected and leave. Do you understand?"

Miles nodded in understanding. –He understood the words, but the rest was more than confusing.–

She was sitting in her usual pose. Her legs were folded crossing each other. She was eating lunch, concentrating on her chicken miso soup, red peppers and tea as she lifted the bowl for a sip and then stopped, sensing something. She slowly took a mouthful of the soup and then put the bowl down, hearing a knock on the door. She was more wary than usual and closed her eyes, trying to sense if danger was behind the door. Rage and Miles were waiting. She sensed no danger. Felling safe, she opened the door, after moving the bowl to the kitchen table. When she put her ear to the door, she heard nothing because Rage had rendered sound outside her door silent to all but Eun.

To her alone, he said, "It's me." Miles mutely watched as the door slowly opened.

Eun saw a tall man in a black and red robe. She wasn't prepared for the unknown today. The arc of her opening door stalled suddenly. Rage, was quick to say, "Eun, Rachel sent me because she couldn't come herself. She needs you. She said you would help. Now."

53

The feeling that something wasn't right was overtaking Eun and Rage knew it. He assured her of the need act quickly, but for Eun, the doubt was unshakable. She had tried, almost quivering, to clear her head. She asked, "Who are you?" This prompted Rage to reply, "I am a friend of Rachel's. She has helped so many, and now she needs your help. I tried, but couldn't. She said you would come to her aid." Rage's influence was swaying Eun to act without thinking too clearly. She agreed to accompany him. Eun said she was ready to go. It was her trusting response to Rage's assurance that he had all that she would need for their quest.

Eun saw Miles as they exited her place. She stopped in her tracks and demanded to know who he was. Rage assured her that he was there to help as well. Miles even nodded pleasantly to her. Somewhat reassured, Eun nodded back. Rage gave her the same instructions that he had given Miles, "Hold on. We will be there quickly."

Seconds later, they all three disappeared from the hall of Eun's apartment building. A flash of lightening had illuminated the dark hallway when they vanished from view.

-9-

Somewhat startled, April was opening her eyes, all the while listening for a confirmation of the knock she thought she heard. Lleangellia knocked again for assurance. April was certain of what she heard and rose from her position in her meditation chair and moved toward the door. From inside, she said, "Who's there?"

There was an immediate reply from Lleangellia, "It is I, the keeper of the birds."

April was reassured and she turned the knob to open the door to a smiling Lleangellia, saying, "Come in."

"We don't have time. We must go now!" Lleangellia said urgently.

Puzzled, April offered to get a few things for their journey, but Lleangellia told her that she wouldn't need a thing. All would be provided. April's face echoed confusion and said, "Are you sure?"

There was urgency in Lleangellia's reply of, "We must go now!"

Chirping from the bedroom caused April to turn that direction and she insisted that she say goodbye to the blue bird. As soon as she has turned away she turned back to see Eve on Lleangellia's right shoulder, chirping happily. April was excited and reached her hand toward Eve. The sweet blue jay left her shoulder and flew to April's finger. April and Eve shared a kiss as April rubbed her little head with her forefinger.

"I hope to see you again. Take care, okay?"

In a flash, the bird flew toward the bedroom, prompting April to warn about the window being closed. Lleangellia was in a rush, assuring April the bird would be fine. She was out the door quickly with April close behind. As April engaged the lock, Lleangellia was heard saying,

"We will be traveling as you have never traveled before. It will be important to remember that you are safe. Even if I am away for a short time."

April was nearly sputtering now feeling frightened and confused, "How will we travel? Are you saying I will be alone?"

Not going into detail, Lleangellia said, "All I am saying is that it will be different. We need to leave now!" Then, there were the remains of a sputter before they disappeared into the clouds. Lleangellia had saved some information for the journey and told April, "I will be going to meet someone else to help with this task. You will be landing in the mountains. There you will meet another person. Do not be afraid. You will be safe while you travel. If I am needed, I will know and I will come." April relaxed and smiled, thinking to herself, "This is amazing!"

Lleangellia wasn't like Rage. She allowed her team to be in contact with each other when she wasn't present. She would have to deliver them one at a time. Now, there is one more. She would be traveling further and wanted them to arrive simultaneously, but it wasn't possible and she settled for the next best thing – almost. She accelerated to her maximum speed to reach the Middle East.

There, Jake was in his office. Even now, he is looking out his window, taking a breather. Within mere minutes of leaving April, Lleangellia has arrived at Jake's building. She is outside his door when he sensed something, and moved toward the door. On the other side was Lleangellia in the same spot as she had been when they first met. The conversation started immediately.

"Hi there," Jake offered nodding.

She returned the gesture and responded, "Are you ready?"

Without giving it much thought, he asked, "For what?"

She reminded him with a flourish, pointing toward the sky, "To help me defeat the one trying to destroy it all."

He feigned forgetfulness, saying, "Oh. I have been praying about this. I wasn't sure if I made the right decision. I think there was an answer, because I felt as if I was told to help."

Jake had thoughts of returning to his home, but the look of urgency that was transmitted by Lleangellia warned him otherwise.

"That which you think you need, you don't."

He immediately understood, "Okay. I guess I am ready."

Rage and his growing entourage had headed toward the last stop before the actual preparation for the battle would begin. Miles and Eun were outside Devon's door with Rage. He had directed Miles to stand to his left and Eun to his right. Framing the door, Rage prepared to knock. The door opened suddenly and its opening prematurely surprised Rage. He backed away, glowing with excitement. Devon stared at Rage.

"I am ready, let's go," spoke Devon.

Devon had moved outside the door, but stopped, a bit startled. He was looking at Eun and Miles. Anxious, he thought to himself, *"How is she going to help?"* He looked to Miles and thought, *"Pretty boy. What will he be doing?"*

Rage knew his thoughts and offered, "These are the others who will be helping. Hold on while we are traveling."

With only moments to spare, all three disappeared, evaporating into the sky.

Both teams saw millions of falling stars that whizzed by, throughout the tranquil night. During the day, they were as plentiful as at night, but unseen. If others had become aware of their presence, disruption and chaos could have been the outcome. It was evidence of how the divine operated. Humans were unaware of their presence. When they were first encountered, humans thought they were having a dream or they are part of a vision. Their minds were incapable of internalizing reality. Some even thought that they had special powers or even a gift to predict the future. It had not advanced though. Human minds tried to find ways to understand. Questions then arose about higher beings revealing themselves, but the beings feared complacency by humans in that case. Their minds seemed to be incapable of handling real truth. There was concern that the world would be turned upside down. The balance could be at stake. Soon, they would be working in tandem – the humans and the higher beings. A lot was at stake.

Rage and his team flew quickly toward the battle. The three had gripped Rage and were clinging tightly as the demoniac moved quickly to the pace where the battle would be contested. Rage warned them along the way.

"Hold on! I need to increase the speed."

It seemed that the speed had doubled. Rage and his team were approaching their briefing locale. Lleangellia's team straggled in one by one.

After what seemed like an eternity, Jesse arrived in the unfamiliar location. It was lush. Emerald green trees were a here and there. They were tall, sporting vines that were long and thick, clinging to the sides of the trunk. The foliage almost engulfed him. Looking beyond that, he could see what looked like a path leading downward. His glance covered the horizon and he noticed mountains behind a grove of trees. Cautiously moving a few paces to his left, he wondered, *"Where is Lleangellia? Why isn't she here?"*

The voice he heard in his head was quiet and calm, *"I am on my way."*

He began to evaluate the scene before him. He tested the vines. They appeared to be sturdy. They were huge…at least five inches in circumference. It was not his usual environment. He reached down to touch the vine and heard a sound from behind. He stopped and listened. It sounded like someone walking through the forest. The leaves transmitted a shuffling sound. He looked in that direction. April was landing. She, too, was unfamiliar with the environs and took small steps, even though she was filled with excitement. She looked at each plant and the soil that surrounded them. She hadn't heard Jesse, until then. She slowly rose and thought she noticed movement from the corner of her eye. He was moving nearer.

The two team members knew that others would be there, but now were unaware of each other. But, they were about to meet. Jake had just arrived, landing between the other two. They were about to converge when Lleangellia appeared. All of them breathed a bit easier; even Lleangellia. She wasted no time in her speech:

"Each of you has been chosen for a very specific and important role. I already explained to each of you that there is an evil, called Norevilania. He has vowed to destroy Earthios. At one point, he was close to fulfilling his wishes. We were

58

able to extract an agreement from him that will prevent him maintaining his control over Earthios. As part of the agreement, you have all graciously agreed to help defeat him. You will need power that will come from deep inside you. He won't be your direct opponent. Just as you were chosen, one of his helpers has chosen his team, too. It won't be easy at all. They will have tricks. All of you will work together; that is the key to victory. Victory will come when two of evils team either thinks of giving up or if two of them actually die. –The same will hold true for us.– We must not give up. The goal will be for them to surrender. Only as a last resort should they be destroyed." Lleangellia was pausing to allow what she herself had said, to sink in. She began again, "You each have special skills that should work in concert. It will help you survive. You must not bicker amongst yourselves. It is essential to work as one. The point is simple, if evil wins, the world will be destroyed."

The three listened intently. They were facing an enormous task. It was sinking in. The seriousness of their faces mirrored their internal vacillation. Jesse relaxed slightly but his stance was strong. Every muscle in his being is flexed with resolve. He was thinking about all his preparation for competition. He had never imagined that he would be using his well-honed body for this. It made his resolution stronger. It was competition; just a different competition than he had planned for. He was ready.

April was usually calm. She always seemed reserved. Now, she was focused on the task at hand. All the years of running away from her earlier trials were making it hard for her to feel anything but fear of reliving the past. She had thought she wouldn't return to that place of fear again. Now she knew she would have to go to her inner well for the fortitude to bring the fighter that was always there back to the present.

Jake was mild-mannered. He had always lived in full view of the world around him. He had no secrets. He understood the significance of what was happening. He knew that his belief would carry him through this. He recalled his recovery from an injury where all the bones in his lower body had been compromised. He knew he was strong.

Lleangellia was listening to their thoughts. She relaxed after recognizing that her team really was strong. They would be ready for what was to come. They would be transported to the battle location. She told them about the journey to come.

"We will be transported to the battle location. You may experience the same sensation as you did traveling here. Any questions?"

The unison negative shake of their heads told Lleangellia that they were as ready as they would ever be.

-10-

Rage and his team arrived at their location. Miles was the first to loosen his grip on the transporter. He was about five feet off the ground when he let go and landed on his feet. He was soon followed by Eun, and soon after, Devon. They were nearly swallowed up by dry, unruly plants and trees. There were rock formations and mountains covered with moss and tall grass off in the distance. They each looked around checking out the foreboding scenery.

Rage planted himself on the ground and watched how Eun, Miles and Devon were responding to the environment. Rage was trying to reassure himself, and he thought, *"I'm sure that it is time to work together to take out Almightanius. I will tell them what to do, they will do it, and it will be good."*

Miles was asking, "Where is Princess?"

Rage bowed his head, knowing just how to play the answer. He said, "She didn't survive. She was brave in battle but Almightanius mutilated her gorgeous body with out provocation. She was a beautiful person that was taken too soon from us."

Rage went on with the heartbreaking story, making it up as he went along. He could see Miles' face. He knew that Miles had been looking forward to having that lovely woman in his life.

Miles was sad. He had hoped upon hope to have another meeting with Princess. He felt as if she had changed his life in the short time that they had spent together, and now he was reeling with her sudden eradication. He was angry. It was fueled by the senselessness of it. It was all the more disheartening to know that she had been taken from him while trying to help someone in need. He was nearly sobbing,

"Why would someone do that?"

Miles was ready to stand up and fight the perpetrator of that evil deed on the spot. He continued, "Let him try and take me out!"

Eun and Devon were confused. Devon asked, "What is he talking about?" Eun examines the situation as she mulled it over and over. She then whispered to herself, "Sad."

Rage wanted to capitalize on the emotion of that moment. He made up the story of Rachel.

"She is dead. Rachel told me that she was going to leave her fortune to you. It is her untimely death that didn't allow her to pass it on to you. She pleaded for mercy, but none was imparted. It is awful that someone who was all about mercy and kindness die that way. Almightanius showed no mercy with Rachel."

All that had made Eun look again at her loss. She raised her head in determination and shouted, "He will die!"

Devon had been watching, but his agenda was different. He was thinking about being the most powerful human alive. Without hesitating, he said, "If we don't defeat Almightanius all that we wish for will be destroyed."

Rage was pleased with the direction things were headed. He was looking at the skies when Devon had ranted his own thoughts. Out of the corner of his eye, he looked at Devon. Devon was focused. It was perfect. Once again, Devon vowed to be a warrior against Almightanius.

Rage offered one last piece of information, "Eun, Miles and Devon, there is one more obstacle. You must move forward and destroy Almightanius. He has gathered a group that has been given the task of destroying all of you. They believe that you are the enemy and they will stop at nothing to annihilate you. If you show mercy to them, you will die. I am making it clear now. Give them no leniency."

The three showed their understanding in different ways. Eun nodded once and Miles shook his head up and down in acknowledgement. Devon, true to form chose an evil grin that was almost a smirk, to prove his understanding.

Rage was confident. He hailed, "They will obliterate Almightanius' team. They will all be no more."

Almightanius sensed that both teams were ready. He transported them to the battleground. Silently, he communicated with

Lleangellia and advised her that they would soon be transported. Then he told Norevilania that his team should be ready, to which Norevilania immediately replied.

"We are ready!"

Rage was informed when Norevilania gave him a final warning.

"Get ready! You are about to be taken to the battleground. It is time."

Rage alerted his team, "Leave NOW!"

The three closed their eyes in preparation.

Lleangellia shouted encouragement to her team too. It was calm when they began their expedition. April, Jake and Jesse closed their eyes in anticipation. Soon they were braced and prepared for the trip. All eight of them disappeared in seconds. It was like darkness being whisked away by a bright light. It was another means of traveling; not the same as when they had arrived.

"We are about to be taken to the battle. Hang on."

The being that had created everything was transporting them. It was the ultimate power with unlimited options that Almightanius possessed. He thought and it happened. In his mind, he had conjured the perfect battleground for the epic battle to take place. It was a far off planet on the outskirts of the Milky Way. It was small and it was unknown. It was much like Earthios. It was the water that made it very different. There was more arable land on the little planet. It was mountainous with an ample supply of rainforest. There were other wild forests. No beings resided on the planet, at least not now. It could be dangerous there. The wild forests had dry and prickly plants that looked like weeds. The plants were entangled. The trees were gigantic, with thick wide leaves and huge trunks and branches.

There were weeds that would confound any gardener. The grasses grew six or seven feet high. All in all, it was challenging terrain. The forest floor was carpeted with vines. There was fluffy moss covering the branches that revealed elongated leaves; different from the other trees they could see. Low hanging leaves made it difficult to navigate the forest. The challenges were not only the opposing team but also the land itself. Almightanius knew this to be true. It was part of his plan.

Almightanius wondered how Norevilania had pulled together the trio of "warriors." *"He should have paid more attention. Would man's skill and knowledge keep creating situations like this? He was saddened at the developments. Norevilania had forced the battle. It was regrettable that the humans were involved, but they were. The battle must commence. Lleangellia is certain that her group will prevail! They must be protected, though. They have frail bodies that weren't constructed to withstand this type of travel. They are not built for this. The orb will protect them."*

Almightanius closed his eyes for a moment. When he opened them again, he was looking straight ahead. Lleangellia and her team, along with Rage and his crew disappear. They were traveling to a place no one knew of, not even Lleangellia. She thought to herself, *"Now it will begin in earnest. Here we go!"*

Norevilania smiled as he sat on his throne. He thought, *"I know that Almightanius isn't happy. I know he doesn't want to be involved in this. He didn't want to bring the humans. He knows they aren't trustworthy. He hadn't a choice, though. We will win. I will do all within my power. I will use every resource to make certain of a victory!"* He was shouting to no one and everyone.

Before they vanished, all were lifted from the ground. Seconds later something that appeared to be a kind of protective orb surrounded the humans. All but Eun looked around in confusion. Rising quickly, the others knew that the battle was about to begin. There was determination on every human face. They were all preparing for what could be their last act – ever.

It was only a matter of minutes before Eun, Miles and Devon arrived at the mysterious location. They knew that their journey was nearly over. The ground that was getting closer and closer looked as if it were grassland. Mixed with it were vines. Miles saw the land as being open. In the distance were several mossy brown mountain ranges. At the foot of the mountains were trees that seem to be a palate of different shades of green. Some are dark; some almost lime green, and some glitter like an emerald. The leaves were wide and thick, hanging just five feet off the ground. The soon to be war-riors were standing close to each other. They looked around and examined their surround, but stood where they had been deposited. Just as Devon turned, Rage appeared.

He told his team, "This is it! The battle will take place here." His group listened as he went over his own plan of action, "I won't be around, but you can call me if you need me. I will be watching over all of you all of the time. I can only intervene if one of you is in dire need though. I will make sure that you have everything you need for a victory. Go and search out the evil ones." It was a rousing speech.

Rage looked at each of his team members individually and spoke privately to each one, looking deep into their eyes, "What you hoped for is not possible because of him. His death will mean that we will all work to help you find another love. Eun, your gift is gone too. And Devon, the only way you will get what you have requested is when he is dead. Each of you has something special to work toward. Miles, your gift is intelligence. It will be essential in tracking the movements of the others. Eun, you have incredible combat skills. No one will defeat you. Devon, you have the skill of influence. All these gifts must be called upon to win. There will be no mercy under any circumstances." No sooner than the last word had left his mouth Rage was gone. He had disappeared from view.

Day one began. Miles was shouting.

"Where are they? Let's take them out. We need to find them now!"

Eun and Devon were supporting Miles, but hadn't said a word. Miles began walking toward the mountain and Eun and Devon followed. A path appeared from nowhere. It was nar-row; only about six feet wide and it led toward the mountains. Vines were moving aside as they walked. Miles was in the lead. He stopped after he walked about twenty yards. He looked ahead and to either side. Devon and Eun stopped, surprised. To the two of them, Miles appeared competent. Miles had sniffed the air repeatedly, and as he looked again to the right there was an area with tall grass interspersed with vines.

"There is something in this direction. I can feel it," he said pointing toward one o'clock from their current position. Devon and Eun had both turned to look where Miles had begun to wend his way through the carpet of vines and grass.

Miles was working hard to pay close attention to where he stepped. He told the others, "Follow in my footsteps! Go this way!"

There was just a hint of hesitation when Devon began to follow along, making sure his feet landed in the exact spot where Miles' had. Each step had the vines scurrying for cover, leaving a clear path for them to follow.

With a bit of hesitation, Devon began to follow along, making sure his feet landed in the same spot that Miles' foot had landed. Each step that was taken was planted on the ground in an open area where there were no vines. It was almost as if the ground knows someone is there. The vines really moved subtly to the side as their footsteps carried them further into the unknown. Miles stopped again. Devon was confused, "What?" It was the first time he had spoken since the three had become a team. Miles said that he could smell something.

He was thinking, "*What made his senses so keen? Do these two have the same abilities?*" He asked them. "Do you smell that?" Miles said looking for validation. Eun and Devon raised their eyebrows in unison, looked at each other, then at him.

"No," they responded almost in unison.

Miles was on the alert. He took a few more steps and stopped again. He looked to his right and stopped yet again after looking toward the ground. There was a bundle in the midst of the grass and vines. It was dark colored with a kind of texture that he had never seen before. It was curious to him. He examined the oddity, trying to see if it was attached to anything. There were vines surrounding it, but nothing appeared to be connected to the bundle itself. He thought he could safely assume that it was not a trap. He began to dissect the bundle. Dead vines appeared to cover what looked like bags. They were rawhide. He showed what he had found to Eun and Devon.

Now very curious, but still cautious, Devon asked, "What is it?" —He had meant to say, 'what was inside the bag?'—

He opened the bag and took a look inside before he reached in to pull peculiar looking, large square objects into the light. He soon realized it was some kind of food. He made the assumption then that the remainder of the bag contained food. Devon was interested.

"What do you think it is?" he almost said to himself and not Miles.

"Food, I imagine," Miles answered.

All the while, he was thinking that Devon should have reasoned that he was looking at it for the first time, too. Curiosity was fueled by thoughts of food. He knew that they hadn't brought any with them, and had wondered how they would sustain themselves. *What kind of food?* Miles bit into the cube. It was familiar. "It is some kind of bread," Miles reported. Devon looked more closely at the cube, which was about eight inches to a side. It was moist, but firm; almost like eating day-old cornbread. Miles was glad that he had found it, because the hunger pangs were beginning to cause more than a mid-sized rumble in his belly.

He gestured to the others, "Actually, it isn't bad. Are you hungry?"

With that, he handed a loaf to Devon. Eun moved closer and Miles gave her another loaf from the leather bag. They ate.

They stood and chewed and swallowed the bread without a word. As if on cue, each glanced here and there, taking in all the terrain and some of the jumbled flora. Miles was looking down when he saw something that caught his eye. It was an oddly curious looking blue vine. All along, he had thought that he could smell water, but couldn't fathom where it could be in this dense landscape. He sniffed the vines because they looked like water. Surprised, he grabbed one of them. As quickly as he had grasped it, he knew. It was the source of the odor, and it was water.

Always a daredevil, Miles had bent the vine until it broke. Fluid gushed out. He tried to detect an odor as the fluid dripped from the vine. He was sure it was water. He let it drip on his tongue, but just for a taste test.

Devon wondered what Miles was thinking by sampling any unfamiliar substance. He was watching Miles intently, searching his face for any sign that he had ingested poison. He finally came to the conclusion that it was harmless. It was water. It wasn't from an expected source, but it would do.

Miles, Devon and Eun were actually enjoying the rejuvenating loaf and the mysterious water from the vine. On the other side of the mountain range, their foils – Jesse, April and Jake had just arrived. The new arrivals were intent on acclimating themselves to the new environment, but Miles, Devon and Eun, had been invigorated by the food and water. They were sure that the others were on the planet. They had an edge. Jesse, April and Jake were still in the process of decompressing from their journey there. It would take some time.

Rage was watching intently, but from a distance. He smiled to no one in particular when he said aloud, "Now Almightanius, you will never be able to claim a victory. We will not be defeated."

As usual, Norevilania was sitting on his throne. Suddenly, as if he was experiencing an electrical shock, he leapt as if for joy and said at the top of his already loud voice.

"Yes! Phase one is complete. They are much more powerful than your measly team, Almightanius, my apparently not so worthy opponent!"

-11-

The moss-covered mountain range the Lleangellia trio was deposited near was different. What the three saw was a forest floor that was covered with an assortment of foliage. It was mostly thick, wide low-lying trees that looked as if they were attached to tall, thicker trees with leaves that were out of reach. Vines grew everywhere, surrounding the tall trees and the small trees alike.

Lleangellia was serious. She emphasized, "We are here now. This is the battleground. Remember what I told you before we left Earthios. The true goal we are striving for is to convince your opponents of the error of their ways before they are destroyed."

Lleangellia had paused to allow the three to internalize the point. Just a breath later, she went on, "You will have everything you need and even more to compete in this skirmish. Some of the gifts may surprise you. It is important to use them wisely. They are the tools of victory. No matter the situation, it is important to remember to keep the gifts from harming each other. That will mean that the battle is lost. I believe in you. Evil will use every trick, every subterfuge, whatever they can find to defeat you. Be on your guard at all times. I won't be able to help you directly, but I will be nearby should you feel you or any of your teammates are in serious danger. You may use your mind to reach out to me. I will know. The planet will give you nourishment. Be cautious though, it could be dangerous."

It was a good thing that Jesse, April, and Jake had listened intently, because there was no warning when she disappeared like smoke that was wafted away with the wind. The three just looked at each other silently. It took a bit of time for them to take in all that Lleangellia had said.

April was scanning the landscape, thinking, *This is cool. I feel at home here.* She looked up and then glanced down to her left. Growing there was a bush that was no more than two feet tall.

It was covered with leaves that were substantial. She wasn't sure what it was. Her gut told her though that it was good for them. It was nourishment. April reached down and pulled at one of the bulky leaves. The bush seemed to shake. She lifted the leaf toward her mouth and nibbled at it.

Jesse and Jake were both looking on with curiosity. They were concerned that it was harmful and they were fearful that something bad would happen to April.

She sensed their approach and said, "It is fine. This is actually food for us. I know it. It is just a soft leaf, and it is good and all I want to do is taste it."

Jesse and Jake watched as she sampled the leaf.

Her eyes lighted up and she said, "It tastes like bread – vanilla bread. It is really moist. Try some. I haven't died."

April offered them each a piece of the leaf. The men turned their portion of leaf over in their hand, examining it for who knew what.

They both chewed on the leaf and soon, Jesse tilted his head back and said, "Not bad. It tastes like a juicy banana." Jake agreed.

April wasted no time in pulling three more leaves from the tree. Noting that it took no time at all to feel satisfied, the three ate and looked at each other, questioning their lack of planning. They had a monumental task to perform and there wasn't a plan in place.

Jake asked, "Where do we go from here?" A lively exchange followed where April professed her confusion and said, "I have no idea."

There was a common theme in the thoughts of the three, "We should have asked more questions." April said aloud what all of them thought;

"We will have to figure it out ourselves. We can, can't we?" The men nodded in agreement. They had eaten their fill and then began to walk toward the mountain range. It was a direction they had agreed on, and having made no actual plans, and it was something – action, not inaction.

Rage and Lleangellia were watching their respective groups consume nourishment before they began their final trek toward the battleground site. They both knew their involvement was to be limited, but they would remain nearby. They couldn't see each other, but they had power that allowed them to be aware of the others' location. They sensed a degree of the other's plight. Rage had maintained most of his abilities even though he had been cast out long ago.

Always looking for the easy, not necessarily right way to do anything, Rage smirked to himself, thinking, *"There has to be a way to intervene. I am sure whatever I do though, her representatives will counter. But then, I am forgetting. She isn't allowed."*

Of course, Almightanius had always known that Rage would be making these attempts. He had given Lleangellia the ability to enhance the abilities of her team, too. She had needed to be a real match for Rage. But, there were limits. He had spent a good deal of time choosing the planet for the battle. It was distant and outside the boundaries of the furthest solar system. The surface of the orb supported plants that would nourish the humans. The landscape was even equipped to enhance their abilities. The mountains had numerous small caves and caverns. Moss covered the mountain ranges but there were many large boulders. The dangers were real, but the six competitors were more mindful than most humans might have been.

The vines were an added deterrent. It made the going slow. The weather was warm, but not too warm. It cooled off occasionally. It was similar to Earthios. That was a plus. The days were compatible, but not quite the same. It would be easy for the participants to find plenty of time to rest and replenish their strength.

The crew members weren't aware of their new abilities. The planet wasn't inhabited at that time, either. It was something that Rage would have changed, because dealing with inhabitants would have further taxed the warriors. Lleangellia was prepared for anything, trusting that her master would do what he could to help when it was needed.

71

Rage's team was still marveling at the water. Miles had his fill and he was presently holding the vine close to Devon's mouth. As Devon's head was tilted to receive the moisture that Miles was trying to deliver by repositioning the vine, the vine gave way. Eun watched as Devon savored the few drops that would provide hydration.

Soon afterward, Devon said, "It is sweet, isn't it?"

She was next and after seeing Devon's reaction moved quickly to share in what the vine had to offer. The three finally felt hydrated. It was a good sign.

Miles stood up when they had finished.

"Are we ready to find the traitors?"

The other two nodded. They were anxious to get started. Miles seemed to be the leader, even though there wasn't a formal agreement that he would call the shots. He began by saying what he had planned.

"Let's continue heading north. We should go toward that really high mountain range. I think it is north."

The other two followed him as he headed toward the mountain, but for just a moment, April acquiesced, but not completely.

"Why? What will be gained?" she asked.

Miles was firm, saying, "I believe that this is the proper direction to begin our search for them. If they are going to hide, it will be in the mountains. If I were to fight, it would be in the mountains. There is protection there."

Eun accepted his point by nodding her head and she joined them in their journey toward the peaks in the distance. The landscape continued to be the same for nearly a mile. Then it began to change. It went from vines, tall weeds and green pear "green" grass on the threshold of a lofty prairie field.

The scenery continued for four or five more miles and ended at the bottom of a draw that was at the bottom of the mountainous area. Miles led the way, with Devon and Eun following close enough behind him. Their marching order had been determined without a word being spoken and no one questioned Miles direction.

There was a similar scene unfolding from the opposite side of the mountain. Jess and Jake deferred when they realized that April was a very capable leader. The food that she had found was important to their mission and with that, she had endeared herself to the two men. They were impressed by her initiative. They felt that her competence could only grow. April began her trek toward the mountains.

The ground was still layered with vines and plants that twined themselves around everything. There were knee high wild flowers everywhere. The ground was layered with the thin, trailing plants. On each side were tall, lean, rustic trees that the vines hadn't forgotten. April assessed the surroundings as she walked. She felt as if she could detect an odor in the air. She moved her head from side to side trying to determine the source. She noticed something a bit more than knee high on the pathway toward her left. She had found something, but what? Jake had been observing April's curiosity.

He spoke right away, "What's up? Do you smell something?

April couldn't suppress her excitement, saying, "Something cool and refreshing, I think."

She left the path then and stepped toward one of the hanging vines. The path had similar vines, but these were slightly thicker and longer. They were tightly curled around the base of the tree. Jesse and Jake had halted their forward progress at the edge of the path. They were watching April. She had reached a slender tree just a few feet off the path.

It was a curious vine and this particular tree seemed a different from the others. The others had just a few vines surrounding them. This tree had numerous long vines surrounding it. April scanned the area. There were a few more of these trees further up the pathway, heading deeper into the forest. It was about six feet tall and she could easily grasp the hanging vines. Her throat was dry. She was hoping for something to quench that thirst. She grasped a vine and noticed that there was a hole at the tip of it.

She was thinking all the while, "*I wonder what will happen if I squeeze it? Will liquid pour out of it?*" She was having a good day. Liquid dripped out of the vine at a moderate rate. Jesse and

Jake's eyes widened with surprise. April slowly tried the liquid with her tongue. As soon as the liquid was detected by her taste buds, she smiled. She exclaimed, "It is good. And, it's cool."

–It was almost as if April knew it would be. She was thinking that she must have acquired some special power that would help the three of them survive in this incredible situation that had forced them together.–

Jesse shook his head, silently marveling at the luck of finding water in a vine. Lleangellia had said that they might be able to do things that hadn't been possible on Earthios. Now, as she offered a taste, Jesse thought, *"How did she know that it was okay? It had been almost as if she could really smell the existence of water. How did that work?"*

April drank and then made certain that both men were hydrated too, offering them separate vines. Jesse and Jake had no problem accepting the welcome moisture that soothed their not quite parched throats. Jesse was remembering what Lleangellia had said, too. –He knew they would have what they needed. So far, it was good.–

They were taking their time drinking their fill from the newly found water-vine. The air that softly blew over them was becoming crisp. April looked around, trying to gain a sense of all that surrounded them. She stopped and then decided to move on when nothing seemed to be amiss.

Jessie asked, "What do you see? Anything?" She was a bit annoyed, but assured him, "I see only what you see. We must continue."

Both Jake and Jesse agreed to move on. They released their grip on the vines simultaneously and then made their way back to the path, following close behind April. She was moving forward; stopping often to take note of anything that might seem out of the ordinary – anywhere in her sight line. Jesse and Jake were paying close attention too. Each of them looked and listened as they strode along. The landscape was boringly consistent. Hiding wouldn't be difficult. Cover was everywhere.

Jesse, being the thorough individual that he was, asked, "Guys, if we do meet or see them, what should we do? I wonder if they will even speak the same language?"

"I don't have the answers to those questions. You must know that by now. My only thoughts are that we need to be prepared for anything. They are out to harm us and everything that we hold dear is hinged on that," she responded, growing tired of the questions, wanting only to be strong enough to deal with what was sure to be coming up in the not so distant future.

The exchange played out, and they continued on their trek toward the mountains. As they moved on, the vines and the stature of the trees changed only slightly. The range was growing nearer. Not only were the vines and the trees changing in appearance, the grass was becoming coarse. That new landscape was opening to a sea of brown grass and very thick shrubs. April was extremely focused. She was watching both sides of the forest as insurance. She had to be certain that nothing surprised them. Jesse was taking up the rear, and he too was in a state of constant alertness. There were sounds now and then, but it was wind moving through the trees and vines that covered the ground.

Watching the two groups as they carried out the unscripted drama was like looking at a reflection.

On the other side of the range, Miles, Eun and Devon approached what appeared to be a ravine that was sheltered by a ridge. Miles walked ahead purposefully. He, like his rivals, was on the alert. Eun and Devon were following, and Devon was checking the scene that was unfolding, equally wary. He was growing curious, *"What is it we are looking for? Do we know if it's a creature, or someone like us, or...?"* The confusion was painful.

Miles liked his leadership role and he was careful with his words. He responded positively, "I'm not sure, really, but what or whoever it is, I think we will be able to have the upper hand."

Eun was becoming more talkative, "I think they will be like us. I can't imagine that Rage would pit us against an entity where we weren't at least equally competitive with them."

The foot of the mountain was about a mile away. They had begun to move up a slight incline that moved up the mountain. The weeds were taller and thicker. Miles continued to walk, assessing conditions as he went. It wasn't long before he noticed something close to the edge of the mountain. It was darker than the rest of the forest floor. It was about three feet off the ground. It was an object that he had to strain to see. He narrowed his eyes and tried to examine it more thoroughly. The others were silent. Miles moved closer to the unusual looking thing, with Eun and Devon close behind. They were looking for movement – breathing, anything. As they moved nearer, it was clear that there was more than one shape. Miles relaxed a few feet away from the object.

Devon, whispers, because he was unsure of why Miles had halted, "What is it? Can you see?"

Miles wasn't sure either, "I think I see bags of something."

Eun has become interested too, tossing out, "They didn't look like ordinary bags. What kind of bags?"

Miles still wasn't sure, but guesses, "They look like some kind of gear bags."

Devon chimed back, "Gear bags?"

Their curiosity was fueled by their mission's purpose. They had all wondered what they would be using in their contest. It wouldn't have been merely wits; each was sure of that.

Miles walked closer to the small multiple mounds. He delineated three separate mounds, when he was able to sort out the stacked camouflaged bags in his mind. He could see that the bags were constructed of dark brown leather. They all appeared to be full. Eun and Devon stood near the bags, watching Miles. He bent down to look even more closely, and soon announced, "It's safe!"

The other two waited for him to liberate the sack's contents. Miles stretched the opening to get a better look. He saw what appeared to be food. It was bread and dried meat. He held the open bag for them to see for themselves, while saying he thought it was food. After a meaningless discussion about the whys and wherefores having to do with someone trying to compromise their safety, Eun suggested that they take the food along and decide later if it was a diversion or some untoward gesture perpetrated by their adversaries, or if it was truly food.

Miles and Devon agreed immediately that they should move on. Both of them were wary; looking here and there; actually expecting danger. The mountains loomed ahead of them. The danger was there. They were sure of it.

April, Jake and Jesse were moving closer to their side of the steep range ahead of them. They had already grown comfortable with their surround and their pace had even quickened a bit. They were on a mission. Anxiety began to rise though as Jake had been spending a good deal of time ruing the fact that he had never been in a real battle prior to this. He was worried about his contributions. Would he be able to help the team reach their goal? He wasn't very experienced in fighting. The only real one he could remember was with his father, and that didn't count.

Lleangellia had heard Jake's thoughts. She let him know, "Everything is as it should be. You will all do fine. The success of a physical battle does not determine a man's heart, or his courage, for that matter. You will be given special gifts that will be the key to our successful campaign. They will be revealed when the need for them is urgent."

April approached the foot of the range with determination and focus. As she moved forward, the terrain had begun to change. There was a slight upward slant that led toward a rocky surface. As the amount of foliage diminished, the color of the rock seemed to alternate between dark red and dark brown. It was different than they had seen earlier in the day. Up the mountainside there were even boulders that moved occasionally, evidently urged on by small earthquakes. Some of the rocks she saw were even rolling down the hillside sporadically.

-12-

Watching a bowling ball size boulder roll willy-nilly down the mountainside, the group was forced to stop and as they did, took in all the plant life. There were small shrubs that looked like cactus; some were miniature pine trees – perfect for Bonsai. The trees had become smaller and shorter as the elevation changed. It was easy for them to deal with the changes, because they had been provided with shoes that were equipped to handle the change. As they ascended further, the number of rock formations increased. It was challenging, but interesting, all the same. Alertness was the name of their game now. They had come halfway up the mountain and Jesse was seeing things, –or so he thought–.

He was mumbling after noticing that a rock had moved. As he approached it, he detected movement and mumbled, "What is going on?" After walking past it, he added –for his own information–, "That was weird!"

April, Jake and Jesse had been power walking and they were halfway up the slope. They were now navigating around huge boulders. Their counterparts had begun their climb on the other side, as well. The terrain was similar to that on the opposite side of the mountain. Each troop had visions that their trek was the most difficult, but in actuality, they were virtually the same.

Miles, Devon and Eun concentrated on climbing the mountain. The angle of the climb was such that they were able to push easily forward without becoming winded by the meandering trail. Many rocks were rolling down the mountain as they moved up. Everyone in the party kept an eye out for danger, because it was their enemy too. The sky was becoming dim, and quickly. Very soon, it was dark. It forced them to end their first day on the far away planet then and there.

April and her team were moving more quickly. They had reached the top of the range and it had revealed a changing landscape. The trees were tall and stout near the edge of the ridge they were using as a guide as they moved toward the mountain. It was making for a difficult trek. Night was overtaking them, and they could barely see ten feet ahead of them. She then made a suggestion that was more than welcome to the other two.

"Let's rest for the night."

Jesse and Jake agreed immediately. They each found a tree and prepared a place to rest. The leaves were thick and each grabbed handfuls of them to use as a mattress. They were soon ready to rest for the night.

Their foils had finally reached the acme of their climb just as the darkness began. There was little light. The sky was nearly pitch black, almost immediately, with little light to even provide a glimpse of the pathway ahead they stopped.
It was far too dark to continue their quest that night. Miles, Devon and Eun agreed to find a place near to each other for their night's sleep. They were quickly prepared to unwind for the night.

Both clusters of humans slumbered soundly throughout the darkness. They all found that the softness of the leaves provided a cushioned bed that encouraged a deep and restful sleep. Tomorrow was another day.

The next morning the sky radiated a light that was nearly blinding. The group leaders, April and Miles, were awakened immediately, each in their own camp. The sun was practically blinding. The others with them began to move more slowly. – Except for Eun who had followed her usual morning ritual and risen early to begin her day with meditation.– The leaders had scanned their camps for danger and had detected none. April had begun to explore the area, setting out first off, to find food. Miles had done the same and while he was exploring, Jake, Jesse and their counterpart, Devon on the other side of the mountain had risen to greet the day, too.

April had begun her exploration to look for food. Earlier, she had scanned the horizon just as Miles was doing the same. Neither had found anything that set off any internal alarms. She had managed to waken the other two after she had procured food and they were soon finished with their morning meal and ready for the day. Miles' crew was on relatively the same schedule.

About twenty yards from where April, Jesse and Jake had camped; the trees began to spread out a bit more. She was looking for danger and any sign of "others". They had reached the top of the mountain, and were heading down now. It was a valley much like the one that they had begun their journey from yesterday.

The valley had numerous boulders that surrounded small alpine-like bushes. Red rocks were covering what appeared to be caves that weren't uniform in size. Some were small; some large, but there were many. April surveyed this new topographical scene. She noticed that the trees seemed to be greener. They were closer to each other too. Jake and Jesse had begun an "explore" too. They combed through the shadows, then the trees, investigating the territory. They were all in awe. She was practically cooing. It wasn't like her at all.

She nearly squeaked when she said, "This is amazing."

All that Jake could add was, "Wow."

They continued to gaze in awe at the splendor of the scenery.

Miles, Devon and Eun had finally reached the top of the range. Numerous trees blocked the view of the valley. The other side of the mountain range was different. Miles was taking the lead and had moved further into the sea of trees that lined the top of the ridge. He was cautiously navigating his way, and as always, watching for danger all the while. The umbrella of trees and the much lower foliage was so thick that it forced them all to practically push their way through. It was only about a hundred yards into the push that their field of vision expanded. It was possible to almost clearly see their way out. The light was becoming brighter by the minute.

April was leading her team through a transitional area on the mountain's other side. It spanned at least three miles, probably more. A virtual hedge of foliage surrounded the ridge. The floor of the valley was about a mile below them. They were descending at a mean forty-five degree angle. It was steep and slippery.

The ground was strewn with boulders that were huge. Evergreens that were spaced five or ten feet from each other were strewn throughout the terrain.

The crew noticed what appeared to be openings to quite a few caves lining the steep mountainside. The entrances were perfect for a human to pass through. The sheer number of the bolder covered entrances made it a curiosity to the impromptu hiker/explorers.

April suggested to her teammates, "Why don't we explore those caves? Maybe 'they' are in the caves since we haven't seen anyone yet."

Jesse and Jake agreed to follow her and they began descending the north-facing mountainside, walking toward the caverns. The three were constantly checking for danger while they were striding along at a rapid pace. They knew the trees would be providing protection from other eyes, and they were on a mission to arrive there as quickly as possible. It was easy to fall in with their leader and move forward.

The six transplanted souls didn't know it, but they were about to have an in person encounter. Midway down the mountainside, about a hundred yards from a cavern's entrance April, Jake and Jesse stood. At the top of a nearby precipice, Miles, Devon and Eun were standing near an area close to the edge that was covered with trees. Miles was surveying the area. Eun and Devon soon joined him. Miles bristled a bit, because he thought he had spotted a peripheral movement. It was just out of the corner of his eye. He looked to the right almost furtively. Nothing seemed to be out of the ordinary. Eun had looked in the direction of Miles' gaze, and had seen nothing out of the ordinary.

Miles spent just a moment to ask himself pertinent questions, *"What did I see? I dare not ask the others. It could be confusing to them. I must wait until I confirm that something is even there. Could it be the others?"* He was now doubly on the watch for anything out of the ordinary, as if anything about this whole endeavor was usual. In reality, there could have been movement.

There in that moment, the starting buzzer they had been waiting for had finally rung. The battle would commence soon. The teams were on a collision course and they were about to make introductions unnecessary.

Jesse and Jake were trailing behind April. They had no idea how close their enemies were then. It was just a short time into their hike before Jake darted behind one of the larger trees. Jesse, acting on pure instincts followed his lead and found his own tree trunk.

The men exchanged questioning glances and even a few words, "What?" Jessie asked.

"What do you see?" Jake had told him he wasn't certain.

April had continued on, not hearing the muffled disturbance behind her. The men watched the ridge for a minute or two and then decided to move on when they observed nothing that seemed to be out of the ordinary. They moved back to their position, trailing April who had just become aware that they were not in her line of sight. She was concerned. Jake and Jesse caught up quickly enough, though. She was now very close to the cavern's entrance.

Curious as to the reasons for the men to have lagged behind, she said, "What happened?"

Jake answered, as he pointed toward the spot where he had the sensation of movement, "We thought we saw something at the top of the ridge, but it was nothing."

Jesse was quick to reiterate, "There was nothing to it, after all."

That hadn't reassured April and she made a slow scan of the entire horizon. Nothing came into her field of view. She was anxious to check out the cavern. It might offer shelter.

"Let's go into the cavern," April had suggested.

In no time they were headed through the clearing and toward the cavern entrance. Jesse gave it one last look before entering the cave. Just as they were passing under the uneven archway of the cavern, he noticed a man. The man was looking in his direction.

"Oh, damn. It's a man," he whispered as he ducked into the little cave.

Miles was the man. He had seen Jesse enter the cave. He turned to Devon who was next to him and said, "There is one of them!"

It was a simple statement that reflected the culmination of part of his reason for being there. He looked toward Devon to make certain he had comprehended what he had said.

Devon was right there, "What do you see?"

"I saw one of the enemy. He went into the cave entrance over there. He was big and muscular. He wasn't carrying a weapon that I saw. I think we can take him out. You know it won't be easy," Miles seemed to be trying to convince more than just Devon. He needed to bolster his own confidence.

Devon wanted more information, "What did you see?"

There was a thorough answer from Miles, "I saw one of the enemy. He went in the cave's entrance. He was a big, muscular guy. He didn't seem to have weapons. I think that if we work together we can overpower him. But it looks as if it won't be easy."

Devon had been thinking, "I don't believe he is there alone."

They decided that it would be best to move as quickly as possible to greet the enemy with confidence and surprise.

Eun was with them, "Let's get him and whoever else there is!"

They were a team and they were heading down the mountainside, but carefully. Miles was keeping an eye on the cave's entrance to see anyone who might exit or enter the hollow space in the side of the supersize hill. He knew that at least one person was inside.

-13-

April, Jake and Jesse were in the cavern. They looked around in awe, surveying the most incredible sights. The cavern opened into a very large vestibule-like area. It was huge. The ceiling was red rock. There were numerous red stone steps that led down to pathways that connected to a bridge that looked as if it passed over a large chasm. The cavern light was dim. They were all surprised to see light coming from some of the rock formations that were cone shaped. Even though the stairs were perfectly constructed without a mark or a crack anywhere, they were odd. They looked newly built and were very steep. They were about a foot wide and each step curved somewhat downward.

Abundant pillars and pylons lined the pathway. They reached to the top of the cavern, two at a time. Just as they met the ceiling, they curved inward. They were tall beyond imagination. It looked like they were six hundred feet high, but it was hard to tell. Rock formations were dripping from the ceiling of the cave. The shapes were varied. They were pyramidal and cubed and conical. It was an odd variety of stone. There was no continuity of size. Some of them were large and others barely visible from the team's vantage point on the trail.

The pathway was an ample distance from the stone of the walls. It led throughout the cavern and appeared to stretch to infinity in either direction, including up and down! The pathway was unusually wide. It was about twenty feet in width. The pillars beside the path to the left were at least 15 feet in circumference. Opposite were pylons of equal size, with pyramidal outer dimensions. The walls were lined with rock formations. Pillars connected the bridges that obscured the darkness that was below. Miles imagined that if one fell they would never return. It was intimidating.

There was a wide gap between the pathway and the cascading stone barrier that complemented the base of the pillars on one side, and on the other were similarly sized but pyramidal based pylons. Rock formations also lined the walls of the cavern. Incredibly tall sandstone pillars not only lined some of the paths, but also connected to the bridges that crossed the dark abyss that was below. Should one fall into the black hole, they would never come back.

Jesse turned around keeping an eye on the rear of the party. They were all listening, and they heard nothing. Jesse suggested that they should move on and not stay close to the entrance. He pointed out that they were easy targets. The other two waste no time agreeing.

Soon, they were heading down the path toward the first set of stone stairs. The stairs were leading them downward, toward a stone square platform on the lower level.

At the platform, the path had options. It continued forward or turned to a much narrower pathway to the left. It was an eight-foot wide path and it led them to yet more bridges and more pathways. They could see three bridges in the foreground. The pathway cut a swath that wove through the cavern's boulders that from their viewpoint actually looked more like large cubes. The cave had a theme in its decorating scheme. The rocks were red. Shades of red were everywhere.

The caves' light was surprisingly adequate. It actually fell in directional slivers from small, round holes that lined the roof of the cave. The unlikely spelunkers were excited to be there. Being in the cave had magically and surprisingly invigorated them. They could see several hundred feet in front of them. Another path was available to them once they crossed the large bridge they had seen as soon as their eyes had adjusted to the light and they had taken in the panorama inside the cave.

Once the lengthy bridge was behind them, they found that the pathway split. It would be necessary to make a choice. To the left, the path continued. It seemed identical to the one they were on, looking as if it connected to a set of stairs that were leading upward, but they hadn't made a choice yet. The trail to the right appeared to lead upward. The now familiar tall pylons were lining the sandy pathway there too.

April, Jake and Jesse were on the steep staircase, each taking it one step at a time, and very carefully, watching intently as they walked, checking for danger at each footfall. It was going well. There didn't seem to be anything affecting their visit to the cavern, even though April had warned them several times to be careful in their descent. It was extremely steep. They were moving downward, unaware that Miles and his cronies were trying to decide where to make their entrance into the cavernous mountain.

Miles asked his partners, "Should we go into the same entrance or try one of the others? I wonder if they eventually end up intersecting somewhere along the way? If we follow them, won't they be quite a distance ahead of us?"

Devon and Eun were anxious to get to the business at hand and both anxiously said, "Let's go in."

They pointed toward the first cave entrance. Not wanting to waste time, Miles turned to his left and entered the cave. It was similar to the cavern that April's team was exploring.

Once inside, Miles peered at the vista. It was incredible. Nothing like this had ever been seen by humans. Miles was dumbstruck by the beauty of it all. Devon and Eun had been a few steps behind him but they soon stood by his side. Its beauty had consumed all of them. The three of them were part of the scenery for quite a long time. They were just taking it in.

The large area had reminded Miles of a rotunda in a capitol building. It was quite a sight. The sheer size was impressive, but there was so much more. It was beautifully landscaped or maybe it should be sandscaped. There were sandstone pathways, stone columns, bridges, staircases and it looked like a small underground city – sans the people, of course.

All that amazement had an affect on each one of them, but Miles brought them back to reality saying, "We need to find them or him or whomever it is we are supposed to be battling."

Although it wasn't an order, it seemed like one to Devon and Eun. They quickly began moving down the steep staircase, intent on their mission. Walking down an incline was always easier than going up. They reached the floor of the cave quickly. There, the path continued left or right but a three-foot stone edging protected the area outside the trail.

Beyond the stone edging, it looked like nothingness. There was no light anywhere. There was a void.

Miles warned them to be careful, "It looks like a serious drop."

Each cautiously descended the stairs, looking left and then right during the remainder of their tedious journey down the pathway. Miles, always in the lead was the first one to reach the diverging paths.

He stopped and quickly decided that they should choose the left path. It was merely a quick step to the left and off they all went trudging silently toward their goal. It was likely they didn't understand the seriousness of this whole adventure. None of them spent much time imagining what the future would be bringing. They just put one foot in front of the other and they moved swiftly and quietly down the pathway.

April, Jake and Jesse had reached the last step of their stairway too.

"We should go to the left," suggested April.

Jesse had been quiet. He finally said, "April, I think I saw one of them before we entered the cave. I didn't want to say anything until I was sure."

"Where did you see 'them'?" April said, unsure of what he actually thought he saw.

"It looked like a man. He was at the top of the ridge. It looked as if he was coming from there. He is either still up there or he is following us," Jesse shared, feeling a little silly for having not said anything earlier.

April was concerned, "If he is behind us, we need to make plans that will keep all of us safe."

Jake chimed in finally, "If it is true, then we need to find a place with protection. We cannot fight now, even if we had a confrontation. We aren't prepared. Beside that, we need to get to a place where we can have some control."

"You're right, Jake. We have to find a new place. Then, we need to make plans. I think we should go to the left now. If they're behind us, we should go right now. We can't be caught in such a risky place," April declared, as she was scanning the cave in the direction where they had entered.

They began walking on the path to the left, as they had planned. Jesse was admiring the wall that was reminiscent of a cascade, but upside-down. There was exotic beauty everywhere. April was focused on reaching a location that would be beneficial for them. It would give them an advantage in a battle. She was striding purposefully down the path, while her brain was working like a computer, sorting through information that might help them all.

They were progressing rapidly as they followed the twists and turns of the pathway as it descended. Jesse looked back to where they had been and he was reassured when he saw nothing that seemed out of place. There was nothing at all to suggest that danger was approaching. The party reached the threshold of the stairs that were spiraling downward. The staircase was winding to the left as it made its plunge to the bowels of the mountain. None of the three hesitated as they maintained their pace and resolutely descended the stairs.

Miles and his party were continuing their exploratory journey down their own pathway and they all vigilantly entered the cave. Miles lifted his head to see if he could determine the source of the odor in the cave. He thought the air smelled of "lilies and stone." Almost as soon as he had identified the odor, he shared his suspicions with Eun and Devon.

"That must be the others. It's as if I can detect humans. And I think they are somewhere nearby."

Miles wasn't the only one who was able to detect individuals who weren't part of his little group.

April had detected something that she couldn't quite identify, but she was growing more and more concerned about the explorers on her team's safety. She quickly decided that she needed to make certain Jake and Jesse were both on board.

With urgency barely disguised, she said, "We must go deeper in the cave. I am sure there will be places where we can take refuge there. We will need more protection than anything I can see near the pathway. It seems as if we are very close to the floor of this cave."

The threesome reached the last step of the winding staircase. It was darker there, but still the foliage seemed unbelievably lush. The area was extensive. It was filled with many stone buildings. The pressure that the three were under didn't allow them to fully grasp the vastness and beauty of the almost familiar, but peculiar sights that were unfolding before their very eyes. It was humbling to try to gain perspective and sort through just the awe of the vastness of their new surroundings.

They decided that they were in an area that was at least an acre. It was an enormous sandy space that seemed more than vast. Options were cropping up everywhere, when minutes ago, they were on a directional path that had consequences that were obvious – step off the path and it would have been the unknown. April was leading them through the trees that were at the edge of the sandy area, to a group of stone buildings. The buildings stood about thirty feet apart. A lot of them were odd looking because they were so tiny. They were almost like cells, quite the contrast to the throne that was the central focus of the area. Jesse had examined several of the small buildings and had decided that they were most likely some kind of meditation chamber.

April had agreed, but was moving forward with Jesse and Jake closely following her. It was as if they were taking an inventory of all that could assist them in the event that the battle would begin when they hadn't much immediate warning. She reminded the men that they had promised to try to convince the others to simply give up and not harm them. She guessed the men would agree, but she said, "The way they seem to be coming after us tells me that convincing them to surrender might not be an easy task."

They walked past the buildings and came to another blockade of vines and trees. There were bushes just past another group of stone buildings similar to the ones they had first passed. Her idea was that they should fan out a bit and not be such a visible or easy target by being together.

Suddenly, there was a shout. April, Jesse and Jake stopped in their tracks and listened. Miles was shouting his demands, "We know you're here! Come out and show yourself."

Rage and Lleangellia were watching the battle unfold. Rage smiled. He was excited. The time was drawing closer for hand-to-hand conflict to begin. He was anxious and he seemed to be giggling like a child. Unaware that Rage was planning to give Eun a weapon, Lleangellia had been watching the interchange between the two groups. She was unhappy with what she saw. She knew what needed to be done, but she was sad.

Lleangellia's team was staying near each other. April whispered to Jesse and Jake that they should move to the next set of buildings. Standing behind the buildings were trees with trunks that would obscure their movements. Still, they were keeping all their wits about them, just in case they might need to defend their positions.

Miles was annoyed. He shouted in a commanding voice.

"Once again, I am ordering you to come out! Show yourself! We need to talk."

While he was giving orders, he was motioning to Eun to move to the left through the trees in search of the intruders. He didn't have to remind either of his partners to stay quiet. Eun and Devon nodded as one, understanding the need to keep their positions unseen by other eyes. As quickly as Eun had performed as she was bid, Miles signaled Devon to move forward through the trees and then down the middle of the expanse in front of where they were standing.
Then, he stealthily moved toward the trees himself.

The massive trees were filled with heavy foliage. There were roots that looked as if they were connected to the vines that were nearby. The vines covered an area that looked to be about twenty yards. They were abutting an area that was strewn with small rocks and lumpy soil. The debris could have been from duplicates of the small buildings that faced the throne. The pillars and pylons that had lined the upper area were identical to those that were near the edge of the floor of the cavern.

Eun was moving stealthily between the trees. She was displaying her skills and it was plain to see why she had been chosen for this project. Rage had done his homework well. She arrived at the edge of the first row of trees, running through the vines and then on to the first row of stone buildings. She reached one of the buildings. It was in the midst of the other buildings. It was a rectangular in shape and it appeared to have an entrance that was about two feet wide and a foot and a half wide.

Eun walked up to the entrance of the tiny space and as she peered inside, she could see that there was a something that appeared to be a weapon. It was nearly three feet long and easily six inches in diameter. There were two grooves that were two inches apart that wound around the lower part of the strange looking weapon. In between the grooves in the object there was an outlandish looking clownish face that looked as if it had a perpetual toothless smile. Even though she felt as if eyes are on her, her scan of the space told her that no one seemed to have taken notice of what she was doing. Miles was ordering the "others" to leave and she used that time to move around the building.

The weapon had found its way into her hands and she seemed quite confident holding it, with what she thought was the business end carefully pointed toward the ground.

Miles moved closer to the small buildings. He approached one very cautiously, looked carefully outside the structure and then he glanced inside as well. He was aware that his sense of smell was guiding him because he sniffed now and then to check for the presence of anything or anyone. There was something lying on the floor of the small building. There, in a covering that was dark and leathery looking, was a sword. It was red with a very thick, long blade. The sword was not as long as his arm. He guessed it was about twenty inches long. The blade was unusual looking. It curved upward soon after the blade left the hilt. He had pulled it out of the scabbarb.

He wielded it with ease. He thought, *"This will make it easy to take out those deadbeats."* He was satisfied that his find would help his group make it out of this place safely.

With that thought, Miles left the building and began to make his way toward the shelter of the trees.

Lleangellia realized that Rage's team was advancing. She knew their intent was to do anything that it took to annihilate April, Jake and Jesse. She closed her eyes and sent a message to each of them. *"Remember that I told you that you all had special skills. If you look within yourself, you will be aware of what those abilities are. It is time to use all of your powers to protect each other and yourself."*

It was confusing for the three to receive the message. They had even closed their eyes to try to detect the source of the voice they were hearing. Of course the other three weren't able to hear Lleangellia's warning, but they stayed vigilant and continued to search for their rivals.

April was contemplating just where she should go, when it came to her. She would just stand up and say what was what and maybe the two groups could move past the impasse that was threatening to cause physical harm to someone.

She shouted, "We must talk about this. Do you even know the truth? We have not harmed you. Why do you want to harm us?"

She was sincere with her words and she had stirred Jesse to raise his voice and plead, "What do you want from us?"

Miles was quick with a response, "You work for a vicious killer. You must denounce your allegiance or suffer the consequences!" –Devon and Eun were getting nearer and nearer to April, Jake and Jesse. They were intent on being able to perform their tasks as instructed. The three would either give up or they would suffer an outcome that could mean their death.–

Jake had always been one to speak his mind. He didn't want to postpone the inevitable, but he could see that everyone wasn't operating with the same truths.

What he thought was needed was a reality check. "Maybe what you were told isn't the truth," he offered, certain his words would incite at least one of the others to think that.

Jesse put forth, "We didn't destroy anyone. Why would we kill?"

April chimed in too, "Let's talk and we can figure out the truth. You have been misinformed."

Miles wasn't having any of it. He shouted back his response, "Why should we believe you?"

He had been moving, along with his teammates, to overtake the other three. Miles was on automatic now. Rage had chosen well. He needn't have worried about the commitment possessed by the leader of his pack of competitors.

April was quietly encouraging Jake and Jess to continue as they had planned. They should move deeper into the cover that the trees and vines provided. She had been trying to get a fix on Miles and finally closed her eyes to get a feel through the unknown while enveloped in what felt like a fog that had been steadily enveloping the challengers, not favoring either of the teams. She realized what Miles had been planning and when she sensed where he was she also noticed another male and a female with some sort of a large stick.

They were all cautiously moving through the densely forested area. Jake and Jesse seemed to be reading her mind. They had seemed sure of what to do, even without her instruction.

Jake said, "I'll take care of the guy in the middle."

Jesse decided to focus on Eun, "I will convince the woman. She may be receptive to my logic."

As it should have been, April knew she would be the one to deal with Miles. Her thoughts were that the two leaders would make their groups' intentions clear, and they would be able to work things out without bloodshed. Wasn't that what had been suggested at the onset of this contest?

Jake and Jesse had decided to stay in the open, hoping that a lack of aggression would make the situation less volatile. Both hoped to avoid a physical confrontation. A truce would diffuse the whole situation. Jesse was walking toward one of the buildings on the edge of the plot where the structures stood. On the backside of the compound, he walked around and visibly poked his head out from the buildings to take a look. He saw Eun. She was coming from the side of one of the buildings, and she noticed him. She stopped and was thinking of what she should do next.

Jesse had moved back behind the building, and he was similarly making plans for his next move.

The two warriors were having a personal conversation. It wasn't with each other; it was with the same for both. It was an internal discussion. Eun tried to will Jesse to show himself again. He was looking at her stick. She was sure she could take him out, right then. He was trying to imagine just how he could defend himself. It was a situation with many possible outcomes. Jesse could feel only one if she used her weapon against him, because he had none.

Defense was the word of the moment for him. He looked around and a few yards from the next group of flora, he noticed a slightly curved branch lying near one of the trees. The branch curved slightly and as Jesse thought about it, it was at least an option. He was unarmed and she wasn't. It was his only option. He picked up the branch and hid behind a tree.

A sigh that Jesse felt slip through his clinched teeth was all that accompanied his find. "It might work, at least temporarily," and that was that.

Meanwhile, Jake, knowing that Devon was continuing his forward movement wanted to complicate his retreat to find a spot where he could comfortably defend himself. He heard a voice behind him as he was inching backward, trying to be alert and maintain his cover. He was expecting to see Lleangellia. It wasn't.

Rage was spewing his viciousness, "Those around you are not going to be of any help. You are alone."

Jake was trying to sort out more than what he could do in the moment, but he was planning what he would do to stay alive. It was a seesaw battle, he was thinking, "*How would he come out on top?*"

Jake was listening, but he wasn't able to discern who was speaking. He reasoned that if it wasn't Lleangellia then it was surely one of the bad people. He had given a lot of thought to taking care of himself, given the last few days. He was certain that he could be an asset to their team, but to what end? He stopped moving forward, to reflect on what it was that he should have been doing. He decided that he needed to find a place where he could feel protected.

Devon had continued his move forward. He said out loud, "This is so cool." He was adept at deceiving others. It was all coming easy to him. It was a gift that was special to him, but not so special to those he came in contact with.

Miles was still droning orders to the entire group, saying, "You are just making it hard on yourself!"

April was focused on forcing him to talk. "Why won't you speak to me?"

Miles was angry and an answer was shouted back at her almost before she had finished the question.

"There is no need. We know what you did and you must pay!" It was Miles at his worst. It was as if he was fueled by adrenalin that lit his rage.

April knew how to force the situation. She saw where he was standing and stepped out, showing herself for effect. She knew it would force a reaction. It was a bold move and Miles looked up in time to see her spin back toward the trees. She wasn't expecting what she saw.

"What the hell?" she mumbled, "He is beautiful. How could someone so strikingly handsome seem to be so evil?" Somewhere in her psyche, she vowed that she would not let his physical magnificence cloud her judgment when it came to battle. She overheard an exchange between Jesse and Eun.

Miles was beginning to have some thoughts that would be abhorrent to Rage. "Maybe I should meet with her," he said aloud to no one in particular.

Eun and Jesse's exchanges were becoming more frequent.

She was taunting him, "Come out, you coward, you."

He was responding to the insults, "A coward – I am not a coward! You don't know me. How is it that you want to kill me without our even exchanging words? Why would you want to do that?"

She had shot back, "It is because of who you serve. That is where the problem lies. I am deeply pained by the thought of anyone serving your master."

95

Jesse was more careful when he selected the next words he threw out. He wanted to make sure he would not appear weak. "I have no idea what you mean. Let's talk. Let there be some reason to our conversation. This is going nowhere."

Eun was irritated at the idea that they could talk. She threw a stone in his direction.

It landed in front of him, and he stepped backward.

"Please. Let's just talk and work this out. We may be quarreling for no reason," Jesse tried to say convincingly.

Eun was acting irrationally, in Jesse's opinion, but he knew she would follow through with her threats.

She taunted, "The only way it will be worked out is after I cut your head from your body and toss it the ground."

The intensity of the argument seemed out of context to what had transpired since the six had begun their face-off deep in the cave. He sighed audibly and was disheartened by the entire interaction. There didn't seem to be anything he could think to say or do to stop the direction of their exchanges. His frustration was growing.

He sputtered to himself, "Why is she doing this? Why can't she be rational?" He noticed a rock nearby. It was huge. He was making a statement, more than he acting on any thoughts that would allow him to change the situation. He picked up the rock, not seeming to notice its weight, and he tossed with ease toward Eun.

The young woman was startled by what was unfolding. The whole incident had caught her attention toward Jesse. She was forced to examine what she had seen.

"That was pretty close. He's got good aim," she surmises. She shouted to him, "There is nothing to talk about!"

Jesse had a look of resolve. He muttered to himself, "Fine!" Then he spoke to Lleangellia and said, "I tried to convince her."

The latter was merely a preamble to what he proclaimed now, "Alright, it's on!"

And it was. There was no time to send messages to their respective teammates. Jesse and Eun prepared to commence their own private battle.

-14-

Devon continued sending subliminal messages to Jake. He immediately focused on reality and he was able to disregard the visual that had been intended to bewilder him. Jake had known where Devon had been hiding. He was mesmerized with the scene that was rapidly becoming a matter of life or death. After all he could swear the rocks were moving of their own volition. Jake and Devon began creeping toward one another.

Meanwhile, Miles and April were nearly face-to-face. Miles had moved forward toward where April was trying to obscure herself. His instincts combed through information from his surround. They were higher than he could remember them ever being. He was trying to sneak up on her, constantly moving slowly, but stealthily toward where he was sure she was hiding. He was sniffing the air, trying to detect her scent. She was watching.

She could close her eyes and see exactly where he was. She moved when she felt him too close. She tried to keep away from him.

"You cannot run forever. I will find you!" Miles had ordered.

April was still hoping to have a dialogue, "You refuse to talk with me."

It was a statement that was supposed to initiate conversation. It could have been the beginning of give and take. In the past, it had always been a good way to diffuse a nasty impasse.

Miles was adamant now. He was intent on the path he had originally begun, and he wasn't moving. "There is nothing to discuss," he shouted to April.

He sounded so unyielding that April was alarmed. She thought it over, searching for a solution that could diffuse the already nasty situation.

She reached out to Lleangellia; "I don't think it's safe to meet him now. I have tried to convince him to talk about our differences. What should I do now?"

April was rewarded with an answer, *"Do what you must. You have tried."* Lleangellia had been more than watching her charges.

Rage had been watching his representatives too, and he sensed that she had given her team unbelievable power and he was irritated to see that she had intervened in that manner when it was against the rules.

Miles stood between the trees and a large patch of vines. He sensed movement and stepped away from the vines, heading toward one of the buildings. He closed his eyes just for a moment, and when he opened them again it was as if a tennis ball sized fireball was being catapulted toward the vine in front of him.

He screamed, "Yes!" It was what he wanted to conjure. He made that ball of fire move to the vines below him.

April was watching. She saw the flaming projectile spurt toward the vines and then flare up when it struck. "What am I going to do now? I am going to try to talk with him one more time. I will take a chance. Maybe if he can see me more closely he will be willing to talk," she thought to herself. She moved toward the furthest away building, keeping in mind just where Miles had been hiding. She was about a hundred feet away from him. Miles could smell her, but he couldn't see her.

Somehow knowing his name, she said, "Miles, please talk to me. I don't want to fight."

She was staying as far away as she could and still converse with him. When he responded though, it seemed a bit too easy. He had been so combative.

She was wary, but hopeful when he said, "Okay, let's talk. Let me see you."

She felt protected against anything that he could do, even though she had seen the fireballs. She stepped out from the shelter of the building. She was beautiful and tried to make herself as non-threatening as possible. Posture was important here. She wanted to appear strong but not a pushover.

Miles was surprised. He had expected to see an ogre or at the very least, a grotesque specimen of the female gender. He was stunned. He wanted to be disgusted, but he was taken with her beauty.

He said, "Since you know my name, your name is?"

She responded softly simply, "My name is April." –All the while she was thinking how handsome he was.–

Yes, Miles and April were having similar thoughts. After all, they weren't so different. Both of them were confident leaders, and unbeknownst to either of them, they weren't operating with the same set of information about their mutual sticky situation.

April couldn't stop thinking, *"Who brought him here? Why did he agree to kill us? What does he think we did?"*

Miles was wondering where she was from. He knew that she couldn't be following the murderer of his precious Princess. She seemed too sweet and soft.

"My name is Miles," he said softening his tone of voice. He couldn't stop with that, "The one you serve was the one who killed my cherished one. I find it hard to believe that you would be allied with one who did that. It was evil and brutal. This same individual destroyed my friends' friend too. Why would you be associated with such a person?"

He had spoken his mind. He was confused and angry, but suddenly he felt in charge.

"I don't know who it is that you are speaking of. The person we are working with would never do anything like that. She is sweet and kind. Birds even like her. I would never work with someone like you are describing. I don't believe in liars and I don't associate with liars or with others who work with liars," she virtually shot back to Miles.

Miles was taking it all in. He was smiling to himself when he took in the whole picture of April. She spoke well. She seemed smart. She seemed strong, and she seemed truthful. That was quite a list of assets. He was mystified by the charges that Rage had listed against her. They were soon within twenty-five feet of each other. Miles thought April was beautiful. She was feeling an infatuation with his mere presence.

Jesse didn't seem to notice the entire drama of the unfolding scenario. He called out to April.

"What is happening over there? What are you thinking?"

Devon looked to his left, hearing the exchanges that were volleying nearby. He wanted to warn Miles. He felt it was his duty to remind him that all these happenings weren't necessarily what they seemed to be.

"Miles! You are being fooled. Remember who she is. Are you crazy? Re-," he started to say but didn't finish, because a rock that weighed more than fifteen pounds was heading toward him. He moved to the side quickly and it whizzed by, missing him by inches."Damn," he finished.

Confusion reigned supreme. Jake and Jesse were distracted because April was distracted. The combatants were in a dither. Each of them was wondering about the others – enemy and colleague alike. It wasn't what Rage and Lleangellia had envisioned as the battle scene. It was taking a turn toward the unexpected. Time would reveal the outcome. But there was more of that to come.

April had tried to convince Miles of her sincerity. She knew that her judgment was clouded by the physical attraction she felt for him. It was confusing.

Jake had tried to move closer to where April was standing, but this had threatened Miles. It was a tense situation. They all knew it.

Miles had finally noticed Jake. He called out to April,

"Did you bring someone here to kill me?" He was angry.

She hadn't seen Jake's new position and said, "No! I didn't bring anyone. It is just you and I." She moved toward Miles, continuing, "Would I get this close to you if I thought you could destroy me? I am not the type to deceive. I am straight up and I am direct."

He knew there was more, but he was enchanted by her mere presence. Her own sensuality was awakening too. They were merely five feet from each other, and it was an old game that they were playing.

Each of them was sensing a desire that didn't seem right for the situation. There was a moment during the encounter where each was so distracted by the uncanny unraveling of the scene, that they forgot where they were. It was a natural emotion that was part of the sexual attraction between a man and a woman. It had very little to do with the critical situation that was at hand.

Miles decided to start over. "My name is Miles," he said politely, but in a strange, tender tone.

She matched the essence of his new approach with a quieter, softer voice saying, "I am April." She tried to look for a way out of their dilemma. All six of them needed clarity. She was deep in thought, *"What are we to do? One of us is supposed to die. I don't know how to go on. If I give in, the earth will be destroyed. If he gives in, then what will I have lost? I am so confused. Is it love at first sight? And if it is, then what does it mean? How can I help how I am feeling? I know that I have a job to do. But, why is it so hard to sort out how to react?"* Confusion was the name of their game. She knew there were no rules; only expectations.

Jesse and Jake had been distracted by April's thoughts. Both of them wasted no time insisting that she remember the seriousness of their mission. They were liberal in their taunts.

"What are you doing, April? How is it that you are thinking about this guy when the earth's future is on the line? How can you be so selfish? Think about all of the people on earth. They will die if we cannot carry out our task. Remember how we got here? Wake up! Now!"

Miles' compatriots weren't waiting quietly in the wings either. Eun and Devon were making sure that Miles knew they were there and they expected him to carry out the missive that Rage had so skillfully outlined for them.

"If you give in to her wishes, we will all die, Miles," stressed Devon. He urged him to kill April and be done with it.

Miles and April were the focal point of all those who were involved in the scene that was playing out deep in the cave. Adding to the confusion, Rage had become irritated with his leader.

Norevilania was snarling at him, "What is he doing? Why isn't he killing her?"

Miles looked as if he was in a trance. He was staring at April and he really didn't quite know what he should do. There was too much at stake to have these thoughts and he knew it. He was trying to understand why he felt such an attraction to her when what he was supposed to be doing was preparing for a battle to the death. It was too much for him to sort through. His eyes began to burn. He was as shocked as any one of the scene's observers at what happened next.

He felt heat from deep behind his eyes. He was sure they could explode. He was concerned about April. She was standing directly in front of him. He turned his head and a huge ball of fire flew from his eyes toward a nearby building. It was a surprise to him. All of this added to his confusion.

April was quaking in the bottleneck that had all her emotions and all the preparation that she had always been certain she could rely on fighting for supremacy. She could hear the caring in Miles' voice, but she could feel the need to live up to her promise to Lleangellia. It was confusing to see Miles turn away from her and then see the reason for that fireball. She was sure that there was more to the events that were unfolding than she could imagine, but why was she feeling so torn between the physical/sexual attraction and the need to carry out a task that could mean the end of something before it could even begin. She could sense Lleangellia.

"April, you must think about what you are doing. You are endangering others – many others. You agreed to something, didn't you?"

Jake was reiterating the sentiments of Lleangellia, saying, "Did you forget about us? I thought we were a team. We are all in this together. We need you with us."

Because it was a team, Jesse wasn't one to be left out. He added, "We can't do this without you."

She looked at Miles and they were of one mind – unsure of their next move, torn between the primal feelings and the reality of each of their quests.

She spoke first, "What can we do? Our comrades want to fight." She knew that he was feeling the same pressure even before he set forth, "I'm not sure. Remember the stipulation that if two die or have significant doubts on one team, then the battle will be over?"

They were being torn by the choices they had and a blow hadn't really been struck.

Jesse spoke adamantly, "April, we are here for a reason. Did you forget? This guy is trying to trick you. Evil is trying to use your emotions to get the better of you. Don't listen to him."

It was difficult, but April did listen to Jesse. She lowered her head. Her expression shifted from the odd state of bliss she had been feeling to sadness and disappointment.

It was too confusing to the potential lovers. It wasn't the time for that. Both knew it. It couldn't be the time unless they carried out their respective charges and lived up to their promises. It was an untenable situation.

Soon he was arguing with Devon. An impasse was building. Even Rage was surprised to know that the infatuation that Miles had with the nymph – the lure Rage had used to lure him – had affected the quandary that Miles was dealing with. His feelings for Princess had transferred to April and he went into protection mode. Rage was not prepared. But he was surely angry.

-15-

The six of them were in a cluster – just not close together. It was an odd encounter. Miles had his attention averted by feelings for April and he hadn't noticed that Jesse had moved very close. Jesse was planning to make a move. He was sure that Miles was trying to confuse April and by doing that, he was out to confound the entire mission. Jesse was certain that he should take charge of the situation and save the day. He reached for a rock without anyone noticing, or so he thought.

April noticed and realized what he was planning to do.

"No! Jesse! No!" was all she could muster.

That had startled Miles and he literally dove forward, landing next to April, but away from where the rock that Jesse had thrown had stopped. It was as if Miles had finally awakened from his lust-induced stupor. He was irritated at April. He began to shout at her.

"You should have stopped him. You knew he was going to do that. That rock was huge. It almost killed me and you just stood there doing nothing."

April wasted no time trying to set him straight. "I didn't know what he was planning. I could not stop him. I didn't want it to happen, just as you didn't." She was frightened and sad that he had so little faith in her, and all that when she had forsaken her alliance with Jake and Jesse for him. She was disconsolate.

There were threats. Miles ordered all of them to leave before he could react to his unhappiness. He even said something horrible, "You need to go before you become residue on my sword!" That was the prelude to Miles' leaving.

She was begging him, "Don't do this. Please. I don't want you to be hurt. You cannot believe that I would do anything to hurt you, or anyone for that matter, unless I was in protection mode. It is not who I am. Please, think long and hard before you make assumptions."

Miles was sad too. He whispered, "This cannot be happening."

April was moving away simultaneously with Miles' orders, but not in response to them. She was sad and confused and Jake was urging her, "Let him go April." She hadn't wanted to, but she did step away. It was painful, but she realized that the golden moment must have passed. She resigned herself to the inevitable. It was over before it started. She didn't even have a handle on the "it". How sad was that? But she knew that was the cue for battle to begin in earnest.

Her tears were falling as she listened to the bickering of Jake and Jesse as well as the opposition. They were shouting taunts that felt to her like playground threats, but it was much more than that now. The future of everything could be decided right now.

One wrong move and it could have been the end for anyone and everyone who mattered to her. But, Miles felt as if he mattered. It was difficult to see him as the hinge. Everything depended on what he was doing now. –Of course, she had no inkling that there were forces beyond even the control of Lleangellia at work.– She knew she needed a moment to collect herself. She wanted to make plans. She needed to convince herself that she could do whatever it took to carry out the mission that she had been entrusted with.

The men were exchanging threats. "This is your last chance," shouted Miles.

"Surrender yourselves!" Jesse was shouting that he had it wrong and that it was Miles' last chance. It was sad to see the warriors appear to be going through the motions and not really living up to the expectations of their recruiters. The overseers were watching with interest and confusion.

Jesse was still using the rocks. There didn't seem to be much of a point to his mission. It was the availability of what he perceived as a weapon. He tossed one near Miles. Miles called him a coward for hiding and throwing rocks. It was sad to see everything sink to such a lowly place.

April was sad. It had been love at first sight, and she meant it. Even though she had only the tiniest of exchanges with Miles, she was in love with him. Her feelings were strong and she knew deep inside her that he felt the same. It was more than depressing. It was miserable to feel the way she did. April was clearing her mind. A deep cleansing breath was first on her list. It was working.

Calmly, she began to take stock. It wasn't just the situation. It was her life. There was too much to take into consideration. The reality she was in the middle of was frightening. She began to peer into the faces of her allies and her enemies. There was more to the scene than the six people. Other things were alive. They weren't human, but they were bothersome in their own way.

The creeping vines were beginning to impede Eun's progress. They were slithering like snakes. Eun was agile and before they could entangle her, she quickly moved away from their grip. It was a dance – like the bunny hop, but with vines. She learned quickly.

Bobbing and weaving wasn't fun. She was more than exasperated. She felt harassed. They were so snake-like that she felt fear as she began to strike out at them. –The scene was being managed by April. She was able to encourage the vines to glide to an area near Eun and impact her movement.– Eun had managed to find a stick that seemed to be in a scabbard. She pulled it out and began striking the viney mass in order to eradicate it. Disconnecting it from the parent plant was forcing it to withdraw and wither with nothing left to give it life.

The vines were increasing their numbers. It had frightened Eun and she had moved nearer to the structures. She was sure that April had some kind of control over the growth of the vines. She didn't know why, but she knew. Just as suddenly as the vines had become mobile, April began moving away too. She was bored and it wasn't really enjoyable torturing the poor woman who looked as if she was practicing for a title fight – all that bobbing and weaving. If it weren't so sad, it would have been comical to see the woman hop her way through the vines that were obviously the aggressors.

Jesse had reached a space that was open. There were more rocks there and he thought they might be valuable in his continuing battle with Miles. The rock throwing had halted and he was preparing to face Miles on a more personal level. He found a sturdy branch. It was three feet long and bigger and stronger than a baseball bat. It was on the ground near where he had stopped to assess the changing scene.

Jesse had hefted his newly discovered and commandeered weapon and it seemed it would serve his purpose. He had heard Miles bellow just then, "I will finally get to finish you off!"

Startled, Jesse was poised and ready for whatever Miles had to offer. Miles had a sword. He was holding it with both hands. Each of the men possessed an air of confidence. They faced each other straight out of some preproscribed duel scene from bygone days. It was Jesse on one side and Miles on the other as they began to circle. Miles was working hard, trying to gain perspective from a physical standpoint. Jesse was obviously the stronger of the two, and space was needed to plan for his moves.

"You deserve to die for supporting a murderer!" Miles spat out.

Miles' anger was a defiant state of mind that projected itself as fury. Not only was Princess, the woman every man dreamed of, taken from him, but also very soon after that, April wasn't even given a chance to be part of his life either. It was unfair. Life was unfair. He was angry, and he was more than disappointed. What was the point anyway? He was turning his inner rage outward. He raised his sword and charged. It wasn't the blow he thought he should strike. Jesse had parried. It surprised him. They moved to and fro almost as if they were waltzing. Time didn't stand still, but they were trading blows with a regularity that bespoke a lengthy battle.

They were using a combination of brawn and wit to duke it out over a something that had never been uttered by either one. Each of them had depended on their benefactors' honesty and Rage was a rotter at heart. He had skillfully disguised his evil intent. He had pulled the three warriors to his side with no reality involved. Deceit was his middle name. He gave treachery not a second thought in his mind. It was all just a means to an end. There was no good or bad; only the goal.

Devon had been trying to have Jake harm himself through some confusion that wound in and out of the reality that was becoming more difficult to sort out.

Jake was working on his own solutions. In his mind, he had been toiling with a huge rock. Suddenly it began to move. He was amazed at the velocity of the rock as it sped toward Devon, who hadn't been aware of his imminent peril. He managed to scoot out of the way at the last minute. The rock landed with a thud where he had been standing. "Whew…" was all he could muster.

It was apparent that he needed to maintain some sense of watchfulness no matter what else was going on. Both men looked away from their tit for tat skirmish and saw that Eun had become determined to eliminate April. They overheard her say, "If I can get close to her, I will finish her off. It will be easy."

April was aware that Eun was out to overpower her. She knew there was more. She was trying to keep things as low-key as possible. She wanted to continue her playful –or so she thought– behavior. It might diffuse an iffy situation. She was working with the vines again. Eun was standing still and April made a vine wrap around her leg. It was climbing, and at first Eun wasn't aware of it. Eventually she was assaulted by three vines that were silently working to halt her progress. When Eun realized what was happening, she looked around and taking a page out of Jesse's book, tossed a rock to change the impetus of the moment. She then began hacking at the vines. Some of them stopped their progress.

She was sure she needed to make a move toward April, and it had to be quickly. April saw the same story unfolding.

She said, "She's moving. I must do the same." That was the plan. She needed a plan of action and she needed to stick to it. She moved quickly and silently about fifty feet from the entrance. She was still standing in the middle of the foliage that had provided cover for all her movements. She was using everything that the greenery provided. The thick carpet of vines, sand and even the fallen leaves muffled her footfalls. She knew that she should continue directing the vines to attack Eun. It wasn't much, but it was diverting Eun's progress, and wasn't that the point here?

April was changing direction and Eun was hacking at the vines. It was drudgery in a battle that had really never gotten off the ground. It was curious to all of them, because they each felt that they were responsible for the ultimate outcome of the skirmishes that so far had been mano-y-mano. She was still controlling the vine's progress and willed it to move faster. Eun's reaction was all she needed to know that she had succeeded. Eun was slashing left and right to try to halt the pace of the vines. April was satisfied that she had not let her earlier dalliances with Miles have an effect on the task they were sent here to perform. Jake and Devon were continuing their confrontation. She peered into the distance and could see that Jake seemed to be doing well, but just then she saw Miles thrusting his sword with incredible force. He was aiming it at Jesse's stomach. It was difficult for her to see, but it also helped bring her focus back to the issues at hand. Jesse had made an impromptu art out of wielding the thick branch that he had armed himself with. It had proven to be a great foil for the red sword that had seemed like it could have magic associated with it, but clearly its power was in hiding at the moment that April was observing the struggle. Miles had managed to meet every flailing parry that Jesse had instituted.

"If I can get that sword, I can pulverize him," Jesse thinks as he blocked each thrust of the sword. Miles wasn't unaware of Jesse's prowess in their encounter.

"This guy is incredibly strong. I cannot compete in these close quarters though," Miles thought. He wasn't going to give up. He was strong and determined. They continued to trade blows – Miles with the sword and Jesse with the self-fashioned club. Their battle was progressing quickly. It had moved nearer and nearer to April and Eun, and none of them seemed to be aware of the other competitors.

Eun's progress had been gaining momentum and she was getting closer to April. April was worried that she was ill equipped for a hand-to-hand duel with Eun. The one thing she was sure of was that she could make the vine continue its attack on her opponent's leg. Eun was so near though that April could detect her breathing. It was nerve-racking for both women. Eun had always been fast and the vines had been the perfect non-violent deterrent. April knew that her opponent was in trouble. If she could just keep the upper hand, it would tire Eun and it could be over and no one would be seriously injured. April had hopes of surviving the ordeal alongside her enemies who would then be allies. She was always a dreamer.

Eun was further enveloped by yet more vines, and now small saplings had joined forces with the creeping vines in the foliage offensive April had launched. It was an all out attack. She was trying to cope with the helplessness that was not her usual companion. She realized that she could conjure up more anger and perhaps break free from the growing feeling of entrapment. She had to react.

Her quickness would have to save her today. She concentrated with all her might, although it was difficult to focus on nothing when there was so much to see and hear and feel. There was much to block out. She finally felt in control and began to chop and pull and cut herself out of the vegetation that was threatening her freedom, or in actuality, her life.

Eun had noticed that when April had lost focus earlier, she then lost the ability to control the vines. She needed to coordinate the two entities – speed at ridding herself of the creepers that were holding her back and she needed to make them stop increasing their numbers. She grabbed a golf ball sized rock. She threw it toward April and as soon as she heard the rock's muffled thud as it hit the ground, she focused on moving toward April as quickly as she could.

April had to scramble backward to escape Eun with her stick. She could see that Eun was angry. Her eyes looked angry. Those eyes looked as if who ever was behind them could kill. It was time to concentrate on saving her very own life. Devon had thwarted another attempt by Jake to sway his sensibilities. Jake hadn't been fooled when Devon tried to instill a vision that encouraged him to bring harm to himself. It was using all the strength he could muster to sort through every image that flashed through his mind. He had to keep reminding himself that he could force the forty-pound rock to "move" as he wished. It was a new skill and he was honing it.

It was Devon who was ducking just in time to avoid the boulder that Jake had mentally hurled at him. It was a shock. Devon feared for his life, and with good reason. He reacted with anger just as another rock sailed in his direction. Jake meanwhile had involuntarily slapped himself in a confusing gesture that Devon had engineered. The battle of minds, or perhaps it was wills, was escalating. The noisy exchange had distracted the others. It wasn't long before Jake moved closer to his adversary. He didn't know if it was for a tactical advantage or some kind of vantage point proximity gain.

Devon had become even more devious with his mind-bending suggestions to Jake. He had projected Lleangellia. His incarnation of her was sending Jake a message that she had lied to him.

He could see her saying, *"I am very sorry. All that I told you is not true. Please forgive me."* This interjection into his thought processes had him examining his underlying motives for even being there, let alone being on track to kill someone he had never met before the encounters of the last several days.

The boulder that was in mid-mind lift fell to the ground. It was obvious to Devon that his directed visions were having an impact. He made more of an effort to convince his challenger that he should surrender. The voice that Jake had at first thought was Lleangellia was telling him, *"You should give up. We can't win."* Jake gave it credence only for a moment. It hadn't seemed like something Lleangellia would have said. He was sure she wouldn't advise him to give up without talking with the others first. Wasn't that what teamwork was all about? And, wouldn't she know that? Of course she would.

The boulder that Jake had lost interest in for a moment had been hanging in the air poised to strike Devon. Refocused, Jake sent the boulder downward. Devon dove out of its path and it missed its mark, crashing instead into a building. But, another huge rock was on its way. Devon was exhausted from the fray. He was drained from the battle. He closed his eyes.

-16-

Jesse and Miles were still exchanging blows. Miles had grown weary with the need to defend himself with the sword. Blocking every blow that Jesse sent his way was growing increasingly difficult. Jesse was aware of his impending victory, he saw Miles turn to run. The branch he had been using so skillfully was on the ground and a huge boulder that weighed a hundred pounds had replaced it. Drawing from stores he wasn't even aware he had, he somehow managed to heave the massive stone toward a retreating Miles.

Miles was watching it move through the area and as he did, he began screaming to April, "Don't let him kill me. I am willing to talk!"

Jesse would have none of it. "It's too late."

Miles was shrieking in fear and urgency. April heard his voice as she watched Jesse telepathically hurl the bolder at him.

"Don't listen to him, I am begging you, April." It was obvious that it would crush him instantly if it continued its spiraling trajectory.

Eun and April were nearby and were still engaged in their own battle. Eun was holding her confusing magic stick high over April's body. She saw Miles and paused for just a moment to take in their unfolding deadly scene. She could see that he was prepared to relinquish all that he had been fighting for so concertedly. He had worked hard to remedy what he believed to be an injustice. She was reflecting on her very own "big" picture. In a split second she had a cascade of thoughts, "*Maybe I can save him. If I do we can win. Revenge will be my prize and I will finally get what I am owed.*" She was distressed to hear Miles cry out and quickly broke her concentration. The foliage was no longer her defensive teammate. They had released their hold on Eun, because she didn't matter any more. All that was in April's head were thoughts of Miles. He was in trouble. She could feel such a connection to Miles. It was a mission that she had taken on without one iota of hesitation. She was overwhelmed by its magnitude.

-17-

Rage knew the victory was slipping away. He would have to intervene. He needed to give Miles more strength and more speed. He was no match for Jesse, physically. And more important, he wasn't a match for April. Rage hated the thought of "love" and he was disgusted with Miles' mewling protestations to April. It was maddening to watch Miles expend all his energy merely defending himself. He thought, *"I must do something. I cannot lose. He will never forgive me."* There was no attacking involved as far as Miles was concerned. It was abominable. Rage was about to intervene when Lleangellia swooped in, both literally and figuratively, and beat him to the punch. She knew what Rage was planning and she wasted no time telling him.

"I won't let you intervene. We agreed to let the humans be the ones to decide. You have already given them more power than was agreed on. You have broken the rules numerous times doing it. I will not let you do more. It will not happen again!" She was livid.

Rage wasn't intimidated. He responded defiantly, "You will not stop me! You are not allowed to fight me. If you do, I will know everything you know and I will have the same power that you have. I will have all of your powers at my disposal. There will be nothing you can do to stop me from manipulating – forever."

Lleangellia was way ahead of him. She had sent a protective shield for the humans. She was sure that he hadn't noticed, at least not yet. It had covered the entire planet. It was a power he did not have and he couldn't penetrate hers. The shield was to prevent any power from entering or leaving the planet. Rage was in the dark. It was her advantage on this one.

Eun moved quickly to position herself behind Miles. She was trying to protect him from being bulldozed by the boulder. It was a matter that required concentration, speed and accuracy working together. She changed the boulder's direction and then she dove from its path. It did slow the boulder, but only slightly. It was just feet away from Miles. Jesse had no second thoughts about the path of the boulder, but he was wishing with all his being that it would destroy both Miles and April. Jesse knew that Eun was behind the altered path of the missile. Eun was focused. She wanted to be there alone. She was sure that she would need no one.

April was watching too. She gazed in horror as the projectile gained momentum. She had to save Miles from a certain and agonizing death.

Jesse was trying to get her attention. He had read her thoughts and was intruding now. He shouted at her, "No, April. He deserves to die."

She reminded him that Lleangellia had urged them to have mercy and not take lives unnecessarily.

She used her powers to come up with a solution very quickly. She could see that Miles was going to be crushed by the boulder. There was no way he would be able to escape its destructive corridor.

Suddenly the vines began gathering. They were moving toward the boulder with such velocity that it surprised even April. Her mind was solely concentrated on stopping the boulders forward movement. The vines had quickly enveloped the boulder and the rock was stationary. In an instant, she was running toward the boulder and Miles beyond. She was sobbing, "Miles."

He looked at her and mouthed the words, "Thank You." The often trite words had never meant more to either of them.

"I did this because I want to trust you. I want you to stop this now!" she thrust at him, her words sharper than a sword to him. She went on, sure that he would listen this time, "It was all because I thought there was something between us. Please, you must stop this ridiculous battle, because you will die and I know that we both don't want that to happen."

Eun still in the arena was watching the scene unfold. She was still intent on her contest with April. All the while, thinking, "I will be so quick. She won't know what happened to her. It will be over before she knows it."

Jesse saw that Miles and April were speaking to each other. Elsewhere, Eun's subtle movements hadn't escaped his notice. It had dawned on him that Eun was intent on hurting April. She was going to attack while April was focusing all her attention on Miles.

That wasn't right. He knew it wasn't a good thing for their team. He moved toward where Eun was perched, intending at first to distract her from her intended target. He was worried about April. He would have to watch out for her more than he had expected. It is as if he has needed to convince himself that his actions were appropriate. It was next to impossible to remain calm.

Jake had never been patient. He was taking in the entire scene as if he were watching a film. The last few days had been a whirl of activity that didn't fit into neat cubbyholes. The mind games and projection or whatever was happening was confusing. He wasn't prepared to see large boulders being flung like ping-pong balls here and there. It was a battle that took a contemporary individual back to the dark ages with its weaponry. But, the kicker was that manipulating rocks and boulders and vines had taken on a new twist. The accuracy was fine-tuned in a way that wouldn't have been possible without the "extra" powers the six were imbued with.

Jake and Devon had been squabbling since their untimely meeting. Each was marching to the beat of what he felt was "right," neither of them taking into consideration that they may have been misinformed by someone who was devious. The situation they were a part of was not ordinary. Their lives had been turned upside down. It was difficult to sort out reality, let alone a manipulated fabrication. Jake's newly found powers had resulted in Devon's death. Jake was suddenly still. He felt as if the wind had been knocked out of him. Now he knew what that meant. He was devastated.

"I have never killed anyone. I am sad. I tried my hardest to change the outcome of this exchange to one of cooperation. To the dead man he said, "You didn't listen. Why? You provoked me. I didn't want this to happen." Tears rolled down his cheeks. His empathy and compassion made him stronger.

Rage was fuming. He croaked at the top of his substantial voice, "Nooo!" That was all he could muster. He knew what Norevilania knew. It was all but over. It was a defeat of huge magnitude. Much had been at stake. It was all hinged on the battle that had nearly played itself out.

The first outward sign of the defeat was that the temperature surrounding Norevilania's throne was rising. His anger at the events on the planet had stifled everything but the heat. Never being one to stand by watching events unfold, Norevilania had a plan. He immediately called on one of his other daemonics and sent them to the preparatory sector, hoping to replace Rage. His last words to the angry, scurrying demoniac was dimension shattering in its volume.

"Get ready to get back in the system!"

Almightanius had destroyed the entryway to the cave system shortly after the agreement had been made between the two. Norevilania was not aware of it. Rage had figured it out the moment that he discovered the impasse that had made it an impossibility to leave the cave, at least by the same way it had been accessed when they entered.

Rage was furious. He had enough to worry about; now the pathway was more than blocked, it was destroyed.

"I know you did something, Lleangellia. I know that you are the one who has made this such a horrible mess." He heard nothing in response, because Lleangellia was ignoring him.

"You coward!" was his response to the silence.

There wasn't a need for Lleangellia to respond. She was calmly trying to maintain an even keel. She didn't want to seem too excited. It wouldn't fit her image. But there was more to her reaction that she couldn't show him. She needed no more histrionics. Even with her back to him, Rage knew that Lleangellia was smiling. –Actually, she was suppressing a giggle, but managed to keep it merely a vision and not a chuckle.–

Miles was explaining to April what he had been told and why he had reacted as he had. It was almost as if he was reminding himself why he had been so angry.

"I have lost too many people in my life. They were special to me. Losing Princess put me over the edge. I was so angry and hurt and confused that when my help was requested I didn't delve into any background. I don't want to die. I don't want you to die. I want to live a long life. And, odd as it might sound at this moment, here, I want to spend the rest of my life with you. The special powers that I was given have made my mind clear. How can we make that happen?"

There was a silence that blotted out other sounds. April was wary, but elated to know that he felt the same as she did. She was thinking to herself how lucky she was that he was on the same channel as she. It would have been a dream coming true in any other lifetime. Today, she wasn't sure what it would mean in the end. But a big piece of her was ecstatic. The other pieces had taken a cleansing breath and were waiting...

Eun had sensed the changes in the scene, but had misread them in her own peculiar way. She was concentrating on her duty. It was easy for her to slip closer to the action with Miles, being the sole object of April's attention. She was within striking distance when she leaned down to find a rock to fling April's way. She was intent on flinging the stone toward April's head.

The "rock" she was searching for turned out to be the size of a softball. It wasn't a rock at all but a lethal weapon. She was lucky that Jesse's eye had wandered. He could see the rock headed for April and if it completed its journey, it would mean the end for her.

Jesse felt helpless. He was sure that April was a goner. There wasn't hope. There wasn't an out that he could see. Suddenly, Miles saw what was unfolding. He had a split second to react. Should he be committed to his teammate who seemed to be at cross-purposes at this point, or should he save April who might be the one he had been searching his entire life for. She was the love of his life. He knew that. Matters were taken from his hands. He saw only a blur and Eun was lying on the ground, unconscious. She still had the stick in her hand and a rock was on the ground next to her head.

Jesse, Miles and April stared at each other for only a moment. April was near tears as she thought, *What was she doing? More important, was Miles trying to distract me?*

Miles was quick with his words, "Jesse saved you. I was about to make my own move when I saw the rock. What a brave and fearless man you are Jesse."

April was still trying to digest the happenings of the last few moments. She was thinking, "Is he believable? Can he be trusted? There is so much to sort through, I just can't be sure of anything."

Jesse sprang to Miles' defense, feeling the tenseness of the moment.

"It is true, April. Miles did look as if he was moving to stop her from attacking you. It doesn't matter now, does it? What will you do, April? I think she is unconscious," he said.

She thought it sounded like a pep talk full of questions. The situation was confusing, indeed.

Jake had wandered over to where the others were chatting. He had his head down. He appeared ready to cry.

Questions were immediately directed to him.

"What is wrong?" April began.

"He is dead. I didn't want to kill him, but my hand was forced," he offered this more matter of fact-like than ruefully. It was a different feeling to kill someone who was trying to kill you. They all knew that. It was a mess. The situation still needed sorting through. It would take a long time."

Jesse was looking at Miles when he said, "One down. One to go."

Miles had thought the situation was diffusing slightly, but that comment told him something different. The situation was still volatile. It could move in any direction and it was essential for all of them to remain calm. They all knew it, but it was not an easy task.

Jake was looking Eun's direction. She was still on the ground; still out. He asked no one in particular, "What happened?" He was pointing toward the young woman's crumpled body.

Jesse quickly briefly and quickly responded.

"She tried to attack April. Luckily I stopped her." Hardly taking a breath, he turned toward Miles, "What will you do now?"

Miles could only think of being with April. It was still strange to him that his need to be with her was all consuming. He was feeling inadequate now, and he wasn't sure just why.

Jesse checked Eun for signs of life. He checked her pulse and then her neck. There was a slight pulse that was discernible through her lukewarm skin. He reported matter-of-factly, "She is alive."

The other three turned to look at Jake, waiting for something. What it was, they weren't sure.

The tide was turning. Norevilania was worried and he told his demoniac to try to destroy Earthios.

The demoniac acquiesced, saying, "I am not sure how."

Anger was frightening when it was coming from Norevilania. He was insistent, "It should be easy! You figure it out! Now! My wishes will be carried out!" Norevilania wasn't seeing a response from the demoniac.

He was aggravated. There was a machine in the room. He made his way to it and frantically tried to access the controls. It wouldn't even begin to function as it should have. He was extremely angry. He was sure that he knew who was behind the malfunction.

Rage was aware of the utter failure of his mission. He knew that going back could be the end of him. It could be the end of everything. Nothing but anger emanated from his view of the fit of rage that was consuming Norevilania. He soon was spewing fire from every pore in his body. It was a frightening sight.

Lleangellia was smiling though. She knew that the end was near. It was a victory. It had been a battle with no predictable end, but right had prevailed. She knew that balance would be restored, and with that knowledge, she knew that Rage would know everything too. He would have to understand that he wouldn't be tolerated by polite society. She was surveying the battle scene.

"Unfortunately, death was part it," she spit venom that accompanied her words. Rage was listening and taking notes.

"You don't care! You and that, that thing that you call Norevilania want nothing but robots; just robots that can't think or choose or empathize. They are all just like you. This is not the end." She was smiling when she finished.
Speaking to April, Miles was almost babbling.

"I don't care. I just want to be with you. I do not want revenge. You are here and I do not want to lose you as I lost Princess. Revenge will never bring me what I want. In fact it will never bring good. I know that now."

Jesse wanted some concrete evidence of Miles' seeming switch of allegiance. "Does that mean you will give up?"

Miles' response was immediate and believable, "I surrender." He turned to April, reaching for her and begged, "Will you be with me, forever?"

Everyone was looking at the two. What an odd insertion into the whacked out scene that had just unraveled over the past week. April the brave leader, the woman who was so strong, was suddenly quiet. Jake was standing.

April had taken a breath before she spoke, "Yes. Yes. I will be with you forever."

Miles smiled, because that's all he could manage without his knees buckling. He and April embraced. They kissed and it was tender. He was exploring her full soft lips. It was apparent that they had lost touch with the fact that they weren't alone. The kiss was sensual and promised more. Their embrace was intense. They reluctantly pulled away from their embrace. Miles was asking, "Now what do I do?" No one knew, or if they did, they were keeping quiet.

Lleangellia was taking in the scene. Eun was lying still on the ground. She was breathing, but not stirring. She said to the group, "You will all return to your world and live out your life." She wasn't invisible to them at that time. She was standing in their midst. "You have saved the world. Your bravery was more than I could have asked for. When your time on Earthios has ended you will have a place in a wonderful world, forever. Your place is reserved. You will return to your lives. You will remember nothing of what has happened here," she directed.

They were all listening intently. They were in awe of her. They all knew they were in the presence of greatness. The group looked as one at Eun.

Jake spoke first, "What will happened to her?"

Lleangellia extended her right hand, palm down. She placed it over Eun. Within moments, Eun was lifting herself from the ground. She was slow. She must have felt as if she was awakening from a dream. She stood up and saw that everyone else was surrounding an apparent apparition. The figure was clad in bright colors. It was a confusing sight to behold. The strange looking figure was talking to her, "No need to be afraid." It was a soft voice and it made her relax.

The others were musing about the oddities of the whole experience on the planet.

Jesse was thinking, *"I wish I could keep this strength."* Before too long, Lleangellia spoke, having read Jesse's mind, "It is a gift that has consequences. You have always been in possession of incredible strengths. They are in many areas. This gift would only confound your world. You have always had what you've needed. You only need to call on your inner strength and you will be equipped to challenge anything that could come your way." Jesse wasted no time conceding that she was correct with her assessment.

She looked at the three teammates. "You will now return to your planet."

She then set her gaze on Miles and Eun and continued, "You chose the path of deception. You will never be the same as before. A small part of you will be lost. You will know that it has disappeared, but only after you have lived without it for a very long time. Making decisions is very important. Miles realized the error of his ways and worked to make a horrible situation have a positive outcome. Miles and April will be able to have a life together because of that. From my perspective, it seems that it will be a lasting bond. It will be up to both to make sure that it does last. Miles, I think I have some information that will make your life easier. Princess was not real. She was actually Rage, and he meant to deceive you with her conjured beauty. You can't have lost her, because she never existed. April however, does exist and you must cherish her always as you do now." That said, she turned to Eun, "You have special gifts. You must use them wisely. The old woman that appeared at your door was another of Rage's disguises. He knew exactly what you wished for and he offered it to you falsely, knowing that he could have you do his bidding if he played up to your frailties."

Eun blushed at her naivety. She was sad that she had been toyed with, but grateful that she was going to get another chance at a good life. It was a life that she had made and she thought then that it could be a very good life. Eun smiled.

"Jake, you have shown your strength. It is clear that you are a valuable asset to any team. You have the ultimate chance to be happy. You have always had the attributes to make it so. You must return to your world and know you are important. It will make you strong," Lleangellia imparted. She had been searching the faces of her "team". She saw what she always had. Each of them was bright and caring. They lived up to their promises. They were good people. They were hard workers. Her mission had been accomplished. She wasn't through speaking, because her current mission was to help them assimilate back into their world. She continued her discourse.

"April, you will have an opportunity for ultimate happiness in your world. It is time to return. Eun and Miles, I want to make you aware that the decisions you make while living the rest of your life on Earthios will determine where you will go when your time there is finished."

She thought she had explained everything, but April's mind was racing. She did have questions. Lleangellia knew the answer before the query could be verbalized, "You will be together. Miles, you and April will not remember a thing about this experience, but I know you will share a wonderful life."

In an instant, Lleangellia had faded into vapor. No one remained. It was as if the beings in the circle had simply vanished from the underground cavern almost as suddenly as they had arrived.

-18-

Back on Earthios, Miles was taking his first trip to the US for a business acquisition. During a brief meeting, he had peeked outside the tower's fifth story window. He noticed a quaint, small park nearby. It looked inviting. A woman was sitting on one of the benches. Something unsaid; something primal; something confusing was whispering to him – go. He knew he needed to meet her. There was no reasoning involved. He didn't question the need. He told the waiting board members that he was leaving, but would return. There was a bit of protest, but he hadn't waited. He simply left the room, entered the elevator and left the building.

Minutes later he was walking toward the beautiful woman sitting majestically on the bench —park where April had met Lleangellia. The lovely woman had long wavy hair and her clothing was simple, yet graceful. She was stunning. It wasn't long before he had stopped in front of her. For him, the view was mesmerizing.

He saw something familiar in her face. He began to wonder why. He was not used to an attraction to a stranger. It was new. He felt week in the knees as he walked closer. He was only a few feet from her when he stopped and stared. It was then that he noticed that her eyes were closed. April sensed the man standing there and she opened her eyes after lowering her upwardly tilted face. When her eyes opened, she saw a very handsome man peering at her. For some reason, she wasn't frightened. Usually, she would have been wary of anyone that close to her. Today, she was surprised to see an extremely well dressed, handsome young man standing just a few feet in front of her.

Miles could feel his emotions getting out of hand. Every sensual part of his body was tingling. He was registering a ten on the intensity scale. He walked toward her. Then, he stopped and stared for a very long time. She was lovely. He was hungry to hold her. He couldn't quite imagine why he felt as he did, but at that juncture, no questions would be extended; and there would be no searching for answers. The woman blushed but she welcomed him when he asked if he could join her on the bench.

As soon as he sat down, he blurted out, "I didn't want to disturb you. I noticed you sitting here and I just needed to say hello. I think you are the most beautiful woman I have ever seen."

He had barely taken a breath before he gingerly took the seat next to the woman. He finished his original thought, "I am not usually this forward, but I couldn't let this moment pass." There, he had done it. He would have no regrets later and wasn't the only one of the five who wasted no time returning to their real life, already in progress.

Jesse had been sleeping. As he awoke, he thought, *"Wow, did I sleep well. I feel really good today."* He was heading to the bathroom soon after wresting his body from the warmth and comfort of the bed. After turning on the light, he looked at himself in the mirror and immediately thought there was someone else in the room.

He was looking for his reflection in the mirror and what he saw was definitely not what usually looked back and thought, *"Who is that?"*

It was nearly impossible that he was the reflection in the mirror. It was his face, but his body was godlike. He was the cover shot of a bodybuilder extraordinaire.

Jesse gathered his gear and was moving out the door. His telephone was ringing. On the other end, a woman was greeting him, "Hi, I miss you."

It was sweet to hear when he had awakened alone. He responded to the conversation, "I miss you too."

Jake was the CEO of his own engineering company. He sat in his office. He was talking on his phone. His life was moving along smoothly. It was curious. He didn't want to think about it, but he knew something was different. He had no idea what it was. It was just different. He couldn't complain. It would have been ludicrous.

Eun had recently decided it was time for a change. She had recognized that her gifts needed to be shared with others. She began her own business and now she was overwhelmed – with success. Her only regret was that she had no one to share it with. She would make that her next project. Life was good. It was going to get better still.

Lleangellia had returned to a heroine's welcome. She had received a head bow from Almightanius. She had already returned to her day-to-day responsibilities. She was monitoring Earthios. She was watching the humans as they went about their business. Three of them were very special. They had brought balance to Earthios once again, and it was a secret. They were all heroes, but there wouldn't be ticker tape parades. But she would always remember.

Lleangellia was happy. Her job wasn't finished, but it was heartening to know that evil would not be in power. She knew that Norevilania would never stop trying to bring evil to her kingdom, but she knew she had helped to prevent it from gaining a foothold. She knew that she would always be committed to that tenet. But it was finished for the day. There would be peace!

acta est fabula